PRAISE FOR ABBY BROOKS

"A masterful blend of joy and angst."

PRAISE FOR ABBY BROOKS

"As a voracious reader it is not unusual for me to read 5-7 books per week. What is unusual is for me to be thinking about the writing and characters long after I've finished the book. With just the perfect amount of angst and remarkable character development, Abby Brooks has crafted a masterpiece..."

PRAISE FOR *BEYOND WORDS*

"Once again Abby Brooks creates a world filled with beautifully written characters that you cannot help but fall in love with."

PRAISE FOR *BEYOND LOVE*

"A lovely story of growing beyond your past, taking control of your life, and allowing yourself to be loved for the person you are."

"Abby Brooks writes books that draw readers right into the story. When you read about her characters, you want them to be your friends."

BEYOND NOW

THE HUTTON FAMILY BOOK 3

ABBY BROOKS

Connect with

ABBY BROOKS

WEBSITE:

www.abbybrooksfiction.com

FACEBOOK:

http://www.facebook.com/abbybrooksauthor

FACEBOOK FAN GROUP:

https://www.facebook.com/
groups/AbbyBrooksBooks/

TWITTER:

http://www.twitter.com/xo_abbybrooks

INSTAGRAM:

http://www.instagram.com/xo_abbybrooks

BOOK+MAIN BITES:

https://bookandmainbites.com/abbybrooks

Want to be one of the first to know about new releases, get exclusive content, and exciting giveaways? Sign up for my newsletter on my website:

www.abbybrooksfiction.com

And, as always, feel free to send me an email at: abby@abbybrooksfiction.com

Books by

ABBY BROOKS

STANDALONES

It's Definitely Not You

The Hutton Family

Beyond Words

Beyond Love

Beyond Now

Beyond Us

Beyond Dreams

Brookside Romance

Wounded

Inevitably You

This Is Why

Along Comes Trouble

Come Home To Me

A Brookside Romance - the Complete Series

Wilde Boys Series with Will Wright

Taking What Is Mine

Claiming What Is Mine

Protecting What Is Mine

Defending What Is Mine

The Moore Family Series

Finding Bliss

Faking Bliss

Instant Bliss

Enemies-to-Bliss

The London Sisters Series

Love Is Crazy (Dakota & Dominic)

Love Is Beautiful (Chelsea & Max)

Love Is Everything (Maya & Hudson)

The London Sisters - the Complete Series

Immortal Memories

Immortal Memories Part 1

Immortal Memories Part 2

As Wren Williams

Bad, Bad Prince

Woodsman

PROLOGUE

Caleb

"I'M GOING to marry you, Maisie Brown."

The first time I said those words, Maisie and I were halfway through Kindergarten. The last time I said those words, I was ten years old, but that didn't mean I stopped believing them. I just got tired of being laughed at for being so sure.

Maisie never laughed at me. Not for swearing I was going to marry her, and not for anything else, either. It was one of the reasons I loved her so much. She and I understood each other. Me with my skinny body—too tall and too thin from the start—and her with her out of style clothes and hand-me-down shoes. Her family never had money, which meant Maisie never fit in and the cruelty of children guaranteed she spent her life watching from the outside, wishing for a place to belong.

(She always had a place she belonged...

...with me. When I was finally old enough to tell her that, she leaned her head on my shoulder and quietly agreed.)

I didn't know she was poor when I was six. All I saw was the shy smile. Those blonde pigtails streaming behind her on the playground. The way her eyes lit up when I made her laugh. I liked making her laugh. It would bubble up from inside and the look on her face was always surprised, as if she wasn't used to being so free.

When I realized she didn't always eat lunch, I started sneaking extra food from home. Mom discovered what I was doing, and after I explained, she started making me two lunches so Maisie never had to go hungry again. That was how I learned what true gratitude looked like. A softening of features. The gleam of unshed tears. A bit of shock and a dash joy.

When the other kids laughed at my stick-figure arms, Maisie took my hand and told me I was perfect just the way I was. And when one of our fathers said or did something awful in an alcohol induced rage, we whispered our stories to each other, heads close, hands held, hearts open.

When I was ten, I told my mother I was going to marry Maisie. Mom gave me a funny look and ruffled my hair. I never said it again after that. Though after we invited her to have dinner with us one evening, I think she saw what I did.

Maisie and I were made for each other.

Our hair was the same pale blonde. Our eyes were the same deep shade of blue. We were both tall and thin, though my issues were genetic and hers had to do with never having enough to eat. We laughed at the same jokes. We loved the same food. And we both swore we wanted to be pirates when we grew up.

The connection went deeper than that, though. It was something my still forming mind couldn't wrap itself around at the time. Looking back, the signs were everywhere. But at ten, all I knew was that I didn't feel like myself until Maisie and I were together. Mom let me invite her over after school, and made sure she knew to help herself to snacks. Dad gave me hell for having a girl as a best friend.

"That's the last thing Caleb needs," he often said, while swirling whisky in his glass. "Hanging out with girls is only going to make him weaker than he already is."

Seventh grade was hard. Maisie's worn clothing stood out even more as the other girls started to pay attention to what they wore. The teasing grew worse, especially when Aiden Stuart was around. My oldest brother Lucas said Aiden had a crush on Maisie, but I didn't believe him. No one could be that mean to someone they liked.

I was tall, but Aiden was BIG. Just an inch shorter than me and already sporting the beginnings of a mustache, the kid outweighed me by a good ten pounds of solid spite. I walked into the lunchroom one day and found him towering over Maisie. He made fun of her hair and called her names and I didn't stop to think.

Dropping my lunch to the ground, I raced across the linoleum, parting a sea of jeering kids as this brick wall of a boy sneered at my best friend. "Roses are red, violets are black..." he chanted.

Maisie tried to shove her way out of the corner, but the asshole had her trapped, with his pack of cackling cronies at his side. "Stop it, Aiden."

"Maisie's chest is as flat as her back!" Aiden shouted the last of the poem, throwing his head back and belting cruel laughter while his sidekicks crowed.

I grabbed his shoulder and spun him around, not even thinking about the world of hurt I was stepping into. All I knew was that Maisie was in trouble.

Aiden glared, fire in his eyes. "String Bean here thinks he can touch me." He turned to his friends, the picture of pure evil. "Did you see that?"

I drew myself up to my full height and squared my

shoulders, hoping to look bigger than I really was. "Leave Maisie alone."

Aiden curled his lip. "Nah." He turned his back, as if to dismiss me, but I wasn't in the mood to be dismissed.

I grabbed his shoulder again. I still didn't have a plan. Distract him long enough for a teacher to show up? Punch him in the gut? Grab Maisie's hand and drag her to safety? Anything and everything was on the table.

Aiden whirled and used the momentum to throw a wild punch my way. It landed squarely on my face, knocking my head back and sending fireworks of pain rocketing through my mouth. Growing up in a household of boys, I'd been pummeled more than once or twice, but I'd never taken a hit like this—one where love didn't pull the punch at the last second.

Stars shot through my vision.

The metallic tang of blood hit my tongue.

And I surprised myself by throwing a punch of my own. My fist connected with Aiden's temple. Hard. He dropped down on the cafeteria floor, a dazed look glazing his eyes.

The laughter stopped. Someone murmured "oh, shit" while someone else screamed "Caleb punched Aiden!" The cry went off across the lunchroom, spreading like wildfire and sounding like victory, but the next thing I knew, a firm hand grabbed my arm and marched me straight down to the office.

The rest of the day happened in a blur of conversations with the principal, my mother's shocked arrival after my subsequent suspension, and my father's clear and evident disdain as they argued over what to do. Mom fought for private school. Or homeschool. And panic rose up inside me at the thought of what would happen to Maisie if either of those things came to pass.

As my lip swelled and I sat with my three brothers at our family table, Dad scoffed. "For God's sake, Rebecca. Stop coddling the kid. The boy has to learn how to grow thicker skin."

I watched his whisky slosh against the glass and nodded my agreement—maybe the last time I ever agreed with my father. "I don't want to go to a different school." My words were slurred around my thick lip and Mom busied herself refreshing my ice pack.

My sister Harlow chose that time to skip into the kitchen, cradling a basket of mewing kittens.

"Look what I found!" She glanced up, the joy melting off her face when she discovered she was downrange of an already agitated Dad.

He threw back the rest of his whisky and thumped the empty glass on the table. "No kittens," he barked, and Harlow jumped, clutching the basket tighter to her chest.

Blinking back tears, she turned to our mom. "But..."

"No kittens! We're running a goddamn hotel, not a daycare." Dad let out a long growl and then stalked from the room, leaving Mom to deal with Harlow's tears.

The day after my suspension ended, Maisie didn't show up at school. She wasn't there the day after, either. I tried calling, but her phone had been disconnected. Dread placed cold hands on my shoulders and I spent the day bothering my brothers by worrying about all the potential problems she might have run into. Wyatt talked Lucas into driving me to her house and what I found there hurt more than my split lip.

Her house had always been a little scary. Small and rundown, with drooping gutters and broken blinds hanging haphazardly from the windows, it looked like the exact opposite of my childhood home. That day, the blinds were gone and a pile of furniture sat at the end of the gravel drive. Mr. Brown's rusted-out truck hunkered under a load of mattresses and bed frames, and Maisie sat on the front step with her head in her hands.

I was out of the car before it stopped moving, feet flying across the overgrown grass. "Maisie!"

She lifted her head and a jolt of fear stopped me in my tracks. Her eyes were red and swollen as tears streamed down her cheeks. Never, in all the years I had known her, had I seen her look so sad, and that was saying a lot.

"Caleb!" She lurched off the steps and into my arms, sobbing into my shoulder, as I awkwardly ran a hand along her back. She cried and she cried while she explained that they were moving. That her dad found a job in the coalmines in Kentucky and was sure things would be better there. "But it won't be better," she finished. "He'll just keep drinking until he loses that job, too. And there isn't a *you* in Kentucky."

The thought of life without Maisie was so foreign, I couldn't process it. From the time I was six years old, I had imagined her at my side until I was old and bent and gray.

"I didn't think I was going to see you before we left." She sniffed as she rubbed her nose with the back of her hand. "They turned off the phone before I could say goodbye." Her parents hated coming to my house. I was never sure why, but Lucas thought it had something to do with money.

I was too young to know what to say as my best friend wiped tears off her face and was hurting too much to do more than stand there in shock as her parents came out of the house and locked the door for the last time. Mrs. Brown hugged me, thanking me for all the times I stood up for Maisie over the years. Mr.

Brown smelled like he'd been drinking and relief weakened my knees when his wife sat down behind the wheel.

"You know how you used to say you were gonna marry me?" Maisie asked, blinking back tears. "Part of me always believed you. Guess the joke's on me."

I shrugged as she climbed into the truck, sandwiching herself between her parents. "Don't be too sure about that." I made a face that I hoped looked brave, keeping it plastered in place while they backed out of the driveway.

Maisie and I stayed in contact for a little while, until one day, out of the blue, their phone was disconnected again. I tried every day for a week. Then waited a week and tried a final time. The number was never reinstated.

And just like that, my Maisie was gone.

ONE

Maisie

AT SIX-THIRTY PM ON A FRIDAY, my plan to escape the office without running into my boss was seriously failing. Every time I thought I was ready to pack up and sneak out, the phone would ring. Or an email would ping. Or someone had a question that just couldn't wait because I was leaving for a much needed vacation tomorrow. Fate had to be sitting somewhere above me, giggling as she flung obstacles my way.

Oooh, look! Maisie's halfway to the door! Quick! Phone call from an irate client! Hmmm...that wasn't enough to get her down. Boom! Coworker with a useless story! HAHAHAHA!

Finally, when all calls, emails and questions had

sufficient answers, I dropped my phone into my purse and plotted my exit strategy. Part of me wondered why leaving work after a ten-hour day felt like a criminal offense, but I didn't have time to listen. If I was going to make a break for it, the time had arrived for the dash to the door. Alas, Brighton Bennett, my best friend at Paradigm Shift Talent Agency and the only other agent with a track record as strong as mine, strolled into my office, looking not worried at all over another lecture from Jacob Lombardi. '*Wedding or not, the two of you leaving the great state of California at the same time is a significant pain in my ass. Blah, blah, blah...*'

Paying no attention as I deflated, Brighton leaned in to study the only thing from my past that still had a place in my new life—a framed picture of me with my childhood friend, Caleb Hutton. His twig-shaped arm thrown around my shoulder, our grins wide, the shot cropped in close so the shack of a house my parents called home wasn't visible behind us. We were blonde haired and freckled, our smudged faces betraying nothing but the happiness we felt when we were together.

After my parents yanked me out of Florida and dropped me into Kentucky, things went from bad to worse. Dad imploded, taking Mom right along with him. Without Caleb looking out for me, I had to pick up the slack myself, or end up following in their footsteps.

Every time something went wrong, every decision life presented me, I asked myself what he would do, and then did exactly that. I modeled myself after him, donning his inner strength like a shield and pulling myself out of that little coalmine town and the dreary future that came hand in hand with the last name of Brown. In a way, I had him to thank for my shiny new life. If it wasn't for all the years he spent fighting for me, I wouldn't have learned to fight for myself, and I certainly never would have learned to fight for other people.

When we were kids, Caleb used to promise he would marry me, and honestly, I always believed him. While fate had different plans for us, (*Oooh, look! She met the love of her life in Kindergarten! Quick! Move her to a different state! MUAHAHAHA!*) in a way, his prophecy came true—just not in the literal sense. His influence was visible in all aspects of my life and my heart would always belong to him. No matter what else fate had in store for me—and if my thwarted office escapes were an indicator, fate had *plenty* in store for me—I would never stop loving him.

Our picture sat in its place of honor on my bookshelf. As the only piece of personal memorabilia I had on display, it stuck out in my polished and professional office, something Brighton made sure to remind me every time she saw it.

"You were such a dirty little thing." She plucked the frame from the shelf and studied it as if she had never seen it before.

Resigning myself to an inevitable run in with Lombardi, I perched on the edge of my desk and fought the urge to check the time. "Isn't that what childhood is supposed to be about?"

Brighton laughed, an easy, breezy sound that was meant to both put me at ease and make me wonder what she knew that I didn't. "Not mine." Her smile would send a triathlete into diabetic shock. "I was all about dresses, bows, and pink, pink, pink when I was that age." Her eyes flicked over Caleb's wide smile. "And boys, too, but my taste always skewed a little more...masculine."

A surge of loyalty tightened my jaw and I opened my mouth to let out a snappy response in defense of the boy in the picture. But, battling Brighton wasn't going to get me out of the office any sooner, so I smoothed my hair back into its no-nonsense (but still highly fashionable!) bun and crossed my legs, bouncing one killer Louboutin-clad foot.

Brighton's fiancé wasn't exactly what I would call masculine, but considering his hipster vibe, he managed to drip power, pride, and money like he had sprung a leak. Anyone who managed to pull that off got major points in my book. What Sawyer didn't have in the old school, alpha male department, he made up for with pretentiousness and passion, which made him a perfect match for Brighton. Personally, I preferred my men a little more rough and tumble. Tousled hair. Bulging muscles. A protective streak wide enough to overpower my independence.

"Sawyer is one hell of a lucky man to be marrying a woman like you."

Brighton turned away from my picture and raised an eyebrow, scouring my statement for any hint of sarcasm. There wasn't any, for the record, but no one in LA said what they meant, so I understood the reaction. "Are you packed? We leave for Key West tomorrow."

"I'm so ready," I lied, offering my friend a genuine smile. Brighton had no idea how close we would be to where I grew up and I intended to keep it that way— my past was my secret.

One night, after too many martinis, Brighton had the swell idea to 'slum it' for her wedding, tittering behind her hand like it was the joke of the century. Always ready to please his beautiful bride, Sawyer stamped the trip with his 'perfectly ironic' seal of approval. After all, who would expect one of the most influential agents in LA to get married on some dingey little island like Key West?

And just like that, Maisie Brown was going home.

Our conversation drifted to the up and coming authors, singers, actors, and musicians all vying for our attention. Even though I was still very aware of the time ticking down on my escape plans, my eyes lit up when she mentioned Collin West, a singer who was about to hit it big. Like, bigger than Liam McGuire before he lost his edge and settled down in Wherever, Ohio.

Collin's story was the best kind. Growing up poor, scrawny, and redheaded, his peers made fun of him for his obsession with icons like Freddie Mercury and David Bowie. After he broke onto the scene at the beginning of the year, redheads everywhere experienced a rare moment in the limelight.

Reversals of fortune, baby.

Nothing better.

Whether we were talking books, movies, or biographies, they were my favorite kind of story.

Proof that nothing about who we are or how we live was set in stone? Yes, please!

Stories showing that no matter how difficult the start, through the right combination of hard work, discipline, sacrifice, or luck, you could end up with everything? Sign me up!

With its wall to wall windows and pristine furniture, my corner office at Shift was a daily reminder of my own personal reversal of fortune.

Of everything I fought for.

Of everything I won.

Of who I became and who I swore I would never be again.

The little girl with a rumbling belly? With ill-fitting clothes and a house in the Florida Keys with no air conditioning? (Let that sink in a moment. Florida Keys. No AC.)

That hungry, sweaty little girl was gone. I grew out of her and into the person I was today. I spent my days glued to my laptop with my phone pressed to my ear, fighting in the trenches to make my client's dreams come true. If I could do it for myself, then I knew I could do it for others.

Sure, I was burning the candle at both ends. And sure, I didn't have a personal life, but the sacrifice was worth it. I didn't even care that I clocked more time at the office than at home, because the view was fabulous.

"You girls all set?" The question came from the doorway and I looked up to find Jacob Lombardi—the man who singlehandedly made Shift what it was today and the boss I had tried so hard to avoid. Salt and pepper hair perfectly matched an expensive suit and a blinding smile reminded us his opinion mattered more than anyone in the industry.

Well, hell.

Cue yet another speech about what an angel he was for letting us use the vacation time we had piling up like dragons hoarding gold. And the crazy thing was, as much as I needed the time off, this vacation wasn't for me at all. As maid of honor, my time would be dedicated to making the bride's week as smooth as possible.

"You know it," Brighton replied while I nodded, purse slipping off my arm as my phone vibrated with a call I'd have to ignore.

Lombardi set his jaw. "Good. Get your asses down there, have a great time, and know that I can't imagine another situation where I would be okay having the two of you out for a week at the same time." He grinned as he repeated a new version of the same thing he'd said for the last month. "So, make the best of it, because it won't be happening again." We all shared a laugh and he offered his congratulations on the upcoming nuptials before heading off to do whatever someone that important did all day.

As soon as he left, Brighton said her goodbyes and followed in his footsteps. I returned a few calls, then checked the myriad social media accounts I adminned before watering the plant that lived on the shelf next to Caleb. It was the single living thing depending on me and a hardy little trooper. Thankfully. I was lucky to remember to feed myself some days, let alone another creature that relied on me for its basic food and nourishment.

"I won't be gone long," I promised. "Just a quick jaunt down memory lane and then I'll be back, right here where I belong." For some reason, maybe because I was talking to a plant as if we were friends, I felt a twinge of sadness that seemed so out of place in my brave new world.

I had no reason to be sad. None at all.

I had everything I ever wanted and then some.

TWO

Caleb

SUNLIGHT GLINTED off the water as I navigated the waves. The smell of sunscreen mixed with the briny scent of ocean air. The engine drone blended with laughter and conversation from the tourists drinking themselves out of seasickness. From the moment I woke up, a sense of expectation had clung to the day. This feeling of something big coming my way. I had no idea what it might be, but I intended to keep my eyes open so I wouldn't miss it.

As a tour boat operator in beautiful Key West, I was always surrounded by people, but never in a way that asked me to do more than smile and wave. I spent my days outside. Stayed true to my need to keep things easygoing and quiet. At best, my impact on people was a stellar vacation memory. At worst, the memory wasn't all that great because of bad weather, but I made up for it by offering them a few more drinks.

Could life get any better?

If I was outside, I was happy.

If I was making people smile, I was happy.

So mostly, I was just plain happy.

By paying attention to who I was and what I wanted out of my time on this earth, I created the perfect life for myself, spending my days on the water and my nights at the bars, or helping my brothers with some project or another at The Hut—the hotel my family owned and operated since I was a kid.

A bikini-clad blonde with the whitest legs I had ever seen stumbled my way. Her tequila sunrise (more sunrise than tequila today—the sun was shining and profit was important) sloshed in a cheap plastic cup in one hand and she clutched her phone in the other.

"Hey, Cap'n," she purred, shifting the device to clutch my arm, then staring in surprise at her mani-cured hand as she gave me a squeeze. "You're so strong." Another squeeze. "And big." She licked her full lips. "I can't even get my fingers around you." She gave me a wicked smile and waited for me to react to her super clever (read: not clever at all) pickup line.

I smiled in return, letting my eyes meet hers, really

connecting in that way not many people were capable of anymore. She flinched away from it, drawing a curtain over her real self by dropping her gaze back to my arm.

"Why thank you," I said, amping up my southern drawl for effect before giving my attention back to the water. (Floridians don't really drawl, but the tourists—especially the bikini-clad kind—didn't seem to care about that technicality.)

The girl practically melted into a puddle at my feet, then asked to take a selfie with me, which she did before I had time to reply, snapping several in a row while pursing her lips, then opening her mouth and flashing a peace sign. She immediately went to work posting the images to approximately three hundred social sites while I navigated us along the rolling waves toward our snorkeling destination.

There were times I felt like I should have been born in another century. A time without smartphones and screen addictions. A time without go, go, go and people getting Instagram famous for the shocking size of their butt. I valued hard work and face to face moments of genuine connection. I was a man out of time, which sometimes meant I was lonelier than I wanted to be.

When you were the only person whose eyes

weren't glazed and glued to a screen, it was amazing how many people thought they were busy doing Really Important Things, but were actually glorified zombies accomplishing not much at all. It's funny how that one difference made me difficult to relate to. But I came to terms with that quickly enough and fostered the relationships that mattered—the ones with my brothers, sister, and mother.

By the time my tipsy tourist finished posting her pictures, it seemed like she forgot why she stumbled over to me in the first place and made her way back to her friends for another round of selfie stupidity. I was happy to see her go. Those super pale legs told me everything I needed to know. The girl wasn't from around here. If her cellphone obsession wasn't enough to make her completely distasteful, then her expiration date was.

I didn't do short-term. Wasn't one for hookups. I looked for depth in a world swimming in the shallow end. My closest friends were sunshine and seawater, and you couldn't get much deeper than that.

We arrived at our snorkeling destination and I went through my spiel, showing my gaggle of fun-seekers how to use the equipment, then watching as they made their way into the water. I found myself tempted to jump in after them. I craved that sudden rush of pressure as the sea closed over my head, the bubbles rushing past my skin as I dove into a secret world, mesmerized by sudden silence. But today, I was Cap'n Caleb Hutton, knower of all things nautical, tourist attraction for the easily distracted. I enjoyed my role and I played it well.

A sudden commotion in the water caught my attention. Splashing. Screaming. Distress. I zeroed in on the hubbub and found a woman at the center, spreading fear outwards in concentric circles. She was firmly strapped into her life vest, so I had very little concern about her going under, but that didn't mean she was safe. Something under the water and out of sight could be the cause of her distress—which meant I needed to get to her as quickly as I could. Without hesitating, I stripped out of my shirt and dove off the boat. With strong strokes, I sliced through the water to where she floundered and wrapped an arm around her waist.

I worked to make eye contact. "It's okay. I've got you."

She met my eyes and I recognized my selfie queen under her facemask. The girl nodded, panicked and wide-eyed, and we made our way to the boat. While she was the one with the life vest, I was the one doing most of the work and by the time we made it back onboard, my lungs were burning and my arms were on fire. I helped her out of her gear and knelt down as seawater dripped into my eyes.

"You okay?" I looked her over for any signs as to what she encountered. Jellyfish? Shark? Ray? There were no obvious signs she needed medical attention.

The woman gasped for breath and pulled her hair over one shoulder. "I can't believe you just dove in to rescue me." Something in the way she ran her gaze down my chest and abs had me growing more and more suspicious.

"Are you hurt?"

She babbled her answer and I struggled to discern what happened, but the picture she drew was clear enough to tell me what I needed to know. A fish had swum too close to her, so close it almost touched her, and...while she tried to sell her fear as genuine, I got the distinct feeling that she had been angling for exactly this reaction from me.

She fluttered her eyelashes and glanced down at her heaving breasts, slick, wet, and straining against her bikini fabric. "I don't know what I would have done if you hadn't saved me."

I helped her to her feet and disengaged as quickly as I could without being rude.

I didn't do tourists.

I didn't do short-term.

I didn't do self-absorbed.

And I really hoped the distress this damsel had manufactured for my benefit wasn't the something big I'd been expecting from the time I woke up.

THREE

Maisie

AFTER THE GLITZ and gloss of life in Los Angeles, the tiki bars and slow meander of Key West had me off my game. For Brighton and Sawyer, everything was 'so ironic' and while I couldn't quite see their angle, I appreciated their happiness. From the moment we stepped off the plane, they seemed, well, exactly as you would expect people to seem on the week of their wedding. At ease, ecstatic, and eager to spend their time lounging half-drunk on the beach.

I, on the other hand, spent my days with my laptop open and my phone in my hand. Sometimes working on both screens at once. Collin West's drive for success didn't stop because I was on vacation—which meant I didn't either. The only reason I didn't have my laptop with me tonight was because Brighton expressly forbid it.

"This is my bachelorette party and you are my maid of honor," she said before we left, with a hand on her hip and a glint in her eye. "I hereby decree that you shall not work and that all work-related topics and accessories are forbidden for the duration of the evening."

The laptop ban didn't stop me from checking my phone. In between taking pictures of Brighton throwing back shots and sipping from umbrella-adorned drinks housed in coconut shells, I got Collin set up with a photoshoot and started negotiating a bit part in a movie.

"Maisie." Brighton leaned over the table and snatched my phone from my hands. "Take a picture with me." The look in her eyes told me that I'd been caught red-handed, so I promised myself I would put my phone away for the rest of the evening. She pressed her cheek to mine and put on her best selfie face—which was fabulous, by the way—and then angled the phone to capture something behind us.

"And just what do we have here?" she whispered, then used her fingers to zoom in on a man sitting at the bar. His tousled blonde hair framed a rugged face, tanned and beautiful with a chiseled jaw and strong cheekbones. A worn T-shirt stretched across broad shoulders and giant biceps. Strong hands enveloped a beer bottle and lifted it to full lips.

Brighton snapped a picture then lowered the phone. "The lighting's shit, but that right there is one fine male specimen." The gleam in her eyes alerted me to a rum-fueled plan of epic proportions. As far as she was concerned, I was going home with that guy tonight.

The image was pixelated, but he definitely checked all of my boxes. Big, brawny beer drinkers were right up my alley. All that testosterone meant they were looking for a hot one-night stand, considering anything more too close to a full-on committed relationship. The muscles usually meant self-absorbed, so I didn't have to worry about anything resembling feelings developing on his end. And, considering my own strong, self-aware nature, the meatheads typically had enough ego to come at me with a strength I could respect. Nothing turned me off more than a beta male.

I'm gonna touch your shoulder now. Do I have your permission?

...shudder...

Brighton sat back down and shared the picture with her equally tipsy sorority sisters, and I took a seat that allowed me space to ogle the man at the bar.

There was something about him...

Something that tugged at a memory...

A sense of nostalgia...

Before I could put my finger on what it was, Brighton and her friends had me walking over to him with a steady, slightly offkey chant of girl-power awesomeness egging me on. Why working from my phone constituted a bachelorette party foul, but a random hookup didn't, would be a question that haunted me for the rest of the night.

Halfway through my journey across the bar, a man stepped into my path. "Well *hello*, beautiful." Drunken eyes struggled to focus on my face, then traveled down to stare with unabashed admiration at my breasts.

While I appreciated the enthusiasm, the man smelled like regret mixed with a heavy dash of body odor and a splash of tequila...just for fun. I stepped out of his way and continued my trek to the bar, hoping the cold shoulder approach would be enough to throw him off.

No such luck.

Sir Stinks-a-lot managed to keep pace with me, invading my personal space and getting more than a little handsy as he rolled through pickup lines with expert level mastery. Not only was I the most beautiful thing he had ever laid eyes on, but heaven must be missing an angel and he knew exactly how to show me such a good time that my toes would be curling into next week.

That one made me pause because *eww*. My utter lack of response up to this point should have been enough for him to take the hint, but it was growing obvious I needed to be more direct. "I'm sorry, but I'm not interested."

One hand snaked around my shoulder, unveiling the full power of the BO housed in those armpits. "That's what you think now," he said as he leaned in too close. "But—"

"She *said* she's not interested." And just like that, my personal space was no longer invaded, my nostrils were free of that terrible stink, and my would-be toe-curler was staring into the angry face of the hunk at the bar—who looked even more familiar up close.

As my savior informed the drunk his time at the bar had come to an end, I studied his profile, trying to understand why he seemed so familiar. I saw a lot of handsome men in my line of work, and a lot of not so handsome men, too. There was a point when everybody looked like somebody. I ran through a list of recent clients to see if I'd found someone's doppelganger, wondering if there was a way the resemblance might work to everyone's advantage.

And that was when it hit me.

The realization came barreling my way, a bowling

ball rumbling down the space-time continuum for a strike, and you literally could have knocked me over with a feather when I understood who I was looking at.

"Caleb Hutton?" I leaned forward, desperate to catch the rest of his face, to erase the scruff and the chiseled features maturity had brought to my childhood friend. "No way. It's really you!"

I waited impatiently as he turned to me, studying me as intently as I had studied him, stripping back the years and the LA polish to find the gap-toothed girl underneath. I got to watch it happen as he realized who I was. The glint of recognition, the dash of disbelief, and then sheer, unadulterated joy.

"Maisie?" He had me wrapped in a bear hug before I had time to reply, hoisting me up so my legs dangled off the ground. "Holy shit! How the hell are you?"

His deep voice rumbled in my ear and I breathed in his scent, this perfect blend of seawater and spice. How had the sweet, scrawny boy I used to know turned into such a stunning specimen of unadulterated *man*? He had been everything I needed when we were kids and now, just looking at him, he was everything I wanted as an adult. Well, physically. The deep love I had for him back in the day negated the 'zero attachment' rule my go, go, go lifestyle required.

I sent out a silent burst of gratitude to fate. *I always knew you were on my side!*

Caleb put me down, walked me to the bar, and signaled the bartender over. "What are you drinking?" He glanced at the umbrella-filled drinks adorning my bachelorette party friends and frowned.

I followed his gaze and chuckled to myself. "I know. I know. It looks bad. But while I may have come from frou-frou central over there, I prefer a few less accessories to my drinks." I turned my attention to the bartender and ordered my favorite—a gin and tonic, top shelf of course.

Caleb lifted an eyebrow when I turned back to him. "Fancy." His gaze drifted down my body, taking in the cut of my dress—casual enough for Key West, but designer nonetheless—the bit of leg slipping through the slit, and the Jimmy Choo sandals dangling off my foot. He liked what he saw, I could tell that much. "You look good."

"So do you! I can't believe you got so big!" With anyone else, I would have tried to come up with a better way to phrase my thoughts, but this was Caleb. There was never a need to censor myself with him, and that had to still be true, even after all this time. The kid I knew hated his thin body. For him to have grown into himself the way he had was good Karma of epic proportions.

He laughed, a warm, throaty sound that went straight to my nether regions, and I found myself leaning in, eager to be closer to him. I caught Brighton giving me two drunkenly enthusiastic thumbs up over his shoulder. I'd have to explain this to her later. The one-night stand was off the table, because this was Caleb and he came with strings attached.

He knew the long, sad story of my past, which I had done my best to leave buried in Kentucky.

He was my first crush, a sweet boy who stood up for me when no one else would, who had grown into exactly the kind of man I couldn't turn down—and still loved with all of my heart.

Even though it felt like fate...

Like serendipity...

Like the most incredible reversal of fortune...

Caleb and I just weren't meant to be more than friends.

FOUR

Caleb

MAISIE LOOKED...DIFFERENT.

And the same.

Her smile still lit up the room. Her eyes still shone with a light of their own. But her hair looked expensive and her clothes looked pretentious, and her friends looked like everything that was wrong with the world. Their squawking and squealing had grown more and more obnoxious as the night wore on. My plan had been to finish my beer and skedaddle the fuck out of there, but, well...

Maisie.

After all these years, she was right in front of me—the something big I woke up expecting. And pretentious or not, she had grown into herself in the best way possible. Blonde hair framed her face, highlighting her blue eyes—the same shade as mine, but offset by thick, dark lashes. Lean and long-limbed, she managed to look both sure of herself and delicate at the same time. With a body shaped by yoga, Pilates, and any number of trendy exercises, very little of the troubled girl I remembered was visible in the way adult Maisie held herself. She looked happy. Healthy. And absolutely beautiful.

"Looks like life is treating you just fine." I found myself unable to take my eyes off her, afraid she might vanish in a puff of smoke if I did.

"Honestly? Life is good right now. It's very, very good." Maisie met my eyes with confidence and didn't flinch away or reach for her phone—though she had it clutched in her hand like a lifeline—as she explained how she ended up in Los Angeles of all places, earning a living making other people's dreams come true. "I didn't set out to be a talent agent, but life kind of navigated me onto this path and I couldn't be happier."

Her phone buzzed and she glanced down at the notification, grimacing as she swiped it away. "What about you? What does life look like for Caleb Hutton?"

"My story is nowhere near as exciting as yours." I gave her the highlight reel, wondering how she would respond to hearing my simple story. Sure, I was a business owner—and a damn good one—but would she judge me for missing out on all the glitz and glam that sparkled around her lifestyle? If she did, so be it, but I would hold it against Los Angeles forever if her spirit had somehow been tainted.

Maisie's wide grin was all the answer I needed. "It's perfect, Caleb. If I was trying to build a better life for you, I couldn't. Out on the water every day? It's you to a T." She sipped at her drink, her eyes locked on mine. "How's your mom?"

"It's been a wild year, but she's good." I filled her in on Dad finally kicking the bucket and the turmoil that followed with my brother Wyatt. "It all ended on a good note though. Wyatt's happy. The family is stronger than ever. And I think Mom's dating." I grimaced, still mildly uncomfortable with the idea.

"Good for her!" Maisie gave a triumphant nod of female solidarity with my mother and the conversation moved on. She told me how hard life had been after her family moved to Kentucky. "I didn't have you there to protect me and things were pretty dark for a while," she said, then apologized for never reaching back out.

I brushed off the apology. "Life has a funny way of leading us down strange paths. We were too young to pull off a long-distance friendship. But you're here now and face-to-face is the best way to do anything."

"It really is." Maisie's phone buzzed, then buzzed

again, then buzzed again. She glanced down, apologizing as she opened her messages and typed out a reply, her thumbs flying furiously over the screen. "This client," she began, but never finished the sentence as a reply came in that had a deep frown tugging at her lovely mouth.

I took a pull from my beer and allowed myself the chance to study her. She was beautiful. Too polished for my taste, but beautiful nonetheless. I mentally erased the makeup and imagined her hair in natural waves instead of styled curls. I wanted to imagine her in shorts and a bikini top, but got distracted with the idea of her naked and then choked on my drink when I realized I was mentally undressing my childhood friend.

Not cool, Moose. Not cool.

When Maisie finally put down her phone with another apology, we lost ourselves to conversation. She ordered a second fancy-pants gin and tonic while I threw back another beer. She leaned closer, placing a hand on my knee, then my arm, throwing back her head in laughter at my jokes. Being with her was as easy as it was when we were kids, but now, she was a woman and I was a man and the pull that always existed between us had a different kind of urgency behind it.

We had chemistry.

And a lot of it.

Maisie licked her lips, her eyes on my mouth, and I did everything I could not to stare at a fantastic pair of breasts barely covered by her skimpy little sundress. The caveman in me wanted to scoop her up and carry her out of the room, laying claim to her because in a way, she had always been mine. Her showing up out of the blue like this was just more proof that she was made for me.

"I have something to say that I've wanted you to hear for years now," she began, biting her lip in a way that made me want to do it for her.

"Consider me all ears, then." With a concerted effort, I focused on what she was saying and nothing else.

Maisie's soft blue eyes touched mine and I saw a flash of genuine gratitude. "I want to thank you for all you did for me when we were kids. It's because of you that I even knew to push for everything I've accomplished, for my freaking amazing life. I mean, who would have thought that me, poor as dirt Maisie Brown, would end up living the high life in Los Angeles, California? Not poor as dirt Maisie Brown, I can say that for sure."

I tried to smile, even though I really didn't want to anymore. Her words tossed reality in my face like a handful of sand. Maisie was here on *vacation*. She was a tourist and I didn't do short-term. For all the chemistry she and I were both feeling, there was nothing waiting for us but another tragic goodbye. In the realm of sobering realizations, this one was a kick to the balls.

"Excuse me..." The bartender angled his head to catch our attention. "I hate to interrupt what seems like one hell of a night, but we're closing. Or rather, we have closed." He gave us a smile and gestured at the rest of the bar.

Maisie glanced at the room behind us, looking as shocked as I felt. The lights were on. Tables were empty. Her friends were long gone, as was everyone else that wasn't an employee. "Did we actually shut down the bar?" She gave me an incredulous grin and hopped off her stool, staggering a little as she laughed. "Whoa. How many of those did I have?"

I wrapped an arm around her and pulled her close, reveling as her smooth skin brushed mine. Together, we made our way out to the street, laughing at the stars and the moon hanging high and clear in the velvet sky. She called an Uber and hugged me goodbye, making me promise that we'd hang out as much as possible before she left.

I stood on the sidewalk for several long moments after she drove away, suddenly aware of the Maisie-shaped hole in my heart in a way I hadn't felt since I was a kid.

FIVE

Maisie

THE SOUND of someone banging on my door half-dragged me from sleep. I managed to lift one heavy eyelid, confused to find myself wearing last night's clothes and sprawled face down on my still-made bed in my hotel room.

"Maisie?" The banging paused long enough for Brighton to call through the door and I pushed myself into a sitting position, pressing a finger to my lips and shushing my friend as if she could hear me.

"I'm coming," I called, regretting the volume of my own voice as my head started pounding in time with an ever more insistent Brighton. "Slow your roll, chica."

When I pulled open the door, she pushed into my

room, pacing and talking a mile a minute, shoving a large cup of coffee into my hands. Her eyes widened as she took in the sight before her. My hair, matted to my head on one side, sticking out like a lion's mane on the other. My dress, rumpled, twisted around my torso, and hanging half-crooked off my shoulders. And one eye, still only half-open, squinting her way like a cross-dressed pirate. "Whoa. Do I even want to know what happened last night?"

Now that she could actually see me, I pressed my fingers to my lips again, closing my eyes as I tried to orient myself. "Please Bri, bring it down a notch. I can feel you talking in my head." I rubbed my temples then took a long drink of my coffee before cracking open a bottle of water and chugging half of it down.

"DRINK MORE. Quickly. I need you at full capacity three hours ago." She blew a slow breath of air through pursed lips, smoothing her hands down the front of her skirt. "We are in full emergency mode, my friend. Like, all hand's on deck."

Pacing my room like an angry little bee, Brighton outlined the reason she was in a panic at the wicked early hour of eleven a.m. (When was the last time I slept this late? Probably the last time I was sick enough to call in. So yeah. I couldn't remember the last time I slept this late.)

"The best man is going home!" Brighton clutched an imaginary throat and shook her hands like she was strangling an invisible someone in front of her. "I am getting married tomorrow and his little hellion of a child has to go and break his arm. Why is the universe so cruel?"

Even through the haze of my hangover, Brighton's lack of empathy stunned me. I frowned up at her, still squinting like a confused pirate. "Yeah." I flopped back on the bed and flung an arm over my eyes. "How dare he go be a good father, concerned about the health and wellbeing of his offspring—hellion or not." I lifted my arm to peek at my friend. "The nerve of some people."

Brighton plopped onto the bed, sending a wave of nausea churning through my guts. "I know I sound awful right now, but come on Maisie. With him gone, the symmetry of the entire evening is thrown off and you know how that bothers me."

I tried to lift her spirits by spewing some line about her now asymmetrical wedding being perfectly imperfect, but she wasn't buying it. She arched one well-groomed eyebrow and pointed at the coffee in my hand. "Keep drinking. You aren't doing me any good with cheesy lines like that."

Cheesy line or not, I wasn't sure what she expected

of me. Did she think I had groomsmen hidden in my luggage? That one text to Collin West would have him on a plane in all his redheaded, under-dressed glory? My mind glommed on to that idea, recognizing it as the beginnings of a plan with potential—as soon as I could drop the pirate act long enough to think straight.

"Honestly," Brighton said on a sigh, "I'm surprised to find you here at all. From what I could tell, things were going swimmingly with your guy from the bar. I was sure you'd still be with him. Though, believe me, I am so glad you're not. Or I will be." She narrowed her eyes and pointed. "As soon as you finish that coffee."

My eyes lit up as the full potential of my plan unlocked. Obviously, Collin was the wrong choice to fill in as best man. He was too famous, too on the rise, and I wasn't ready to start calling in favors with him yet.

I sat up, my smile growing as I looked at my friend. Brighton gave me a knowing grin. "You've got an idea, don't you? Quick." She waved her hands in my direction. "Chug the rest of your coffee before you lose it."

As I forced down the bitter drink, the idea formed fully. And even I had to admit, it was sublime. The right choice had been presented to me last night in all his kind and mind-numbingly handsome glory.

And the best part?

I knew he would do it.

I knew he would put his plans on hold to don a tuxedo and spend a night celebrating with strangers because that's the kind of man Caleb Hutton was.

Though...wait...

That wasn't the best part.

Not by a long shot.

The truly best part was that if Caleb filled in for the best man, he would be my partner for the evening. We would have a reason to spend many hours together —decked out in evening wear no less.

I missed him. And finding him again felt like a singular gift, tossed down from the heavens to enjoy before the clock ticked down on this little vacation and we went back to living on opposite ends of the country. And one thing I learned without question, growing up as poor as I did, if someone was tossing gifts your way, grab 'em up, say thank you, and figure out how to make it last.

SIX

Caleb

WHEN WE WERE LITTLE, Maisie's laugh always seemed to surprise her, as if she didn't know laughter was a feature that came preinstalled with the human condition. At the bar last night, she laughed easily, her smile light, her eyes clear. Everything about her, the way she spoke, the way she moved, it all told me that life was better for her than it had been in childhood, and I was glad she had figured out what she needed. There was no doubt in my mind that she was the one who made it happen. Some people wandered into luck, but not Maisie. Somehow, I knew she had created everything I ever wanted for her out of nothing but grit and determination.

Today was a scorcher, but the breeze off the water was fresh and the tourists in my care were happy. While I was out too late with Maisie the night before, my energy was high, even if I was a little distracted by the scandalous way that sundress looked on her body. For as many times as I tried to focus on earning the money my clients spent on my time, I found my thoughts wandering back to her.

Even being as distracted as I was, I managed to make it back to the marina without having to dive into the water for any unneeded rescues. While I might not have been my usual, engaged self, everyone seemed to have a great day in their facemasks and life vests. Definitely a win in my book. As tourists filtered off my boat with giant grins and plenty of gratitude, I sat back, smiling. Life was good. Life was very, very good. And with Maisie around, it was only going to get better.

I finished docking the boat and whipped out my flip phone to shoot my brother Wyatt a text, wanting to set up a time Maisie and I could have dinner at The Hut with my family. She spent so much time with us when we were kids that she might as well sport the Hutton name herself. And while younger me had always assumed that was how life would work out, older me was just happy to have found her again.

Before I even managed to tap out word one in my message to Wyatt, someone interrupted me. "What is this, two thousand and four?" Humor graced a feminine voice and I knew who I was talking to before I even looked up. "You know technology has left you in the dust, right? I feel like it's my duty as your friend to let you know that you look a little ridiculous right now."

I flipped my phone shut and shoved it into one of the many pockets of my cargo shorts, looking up to find a grinning Maisie. Another sundress graced her body, leaving her shoulders bare, her long neck looking perfectly kissable. "Good afternoon to you, too."

She looped her arm through mine. "Walk with me, Hutton. I have a proposition for you."

A hundred different lewd thoughts leapt to their feet, begging for attention, but I returned them to where they belonged—a dirty little box in the back of my mind. "That's funny, because I have a proposition for you, too." I focused hard on my idea to invite Maisie to dinner at The Hut to give her a chance to reconnect with her past and show off how far she had come. Pure, simple thoughts that had nothing to do with that sundress finding its way to my bedroom floor. Or those full lips wrapped around my—

"I doubt we're thinking about the same thing." She gave me a wicked smile.

And...welcome back lewd thoughts.

Though, as Maisie launched into her idea, that line

of thinking settled down into a disappointed lump of 'not gonna happen, Moose.'

"Let me get this straight," I said, coming to a stop and pulling my arm from hers. "You want me to fill in as best man for your friend's wedding. A wedding that is happening tomorrow afternoon, where I will know exactly zero people other than you."

"Sounds awesome, right?" The wind off the ocean blew Maisie's hair across her face and she delicately tucked it behind her ear. She wore it straight today and it hung in a perfect curtain down her back. "Free food and booze. A chance to dress up. And the best part? We can spend the entire night together, people watching and enjoying said free food and booze."

"When you put it that way, I can't think of a better way to dread a Saturday afternoon." I wrapped an arm around Maisie's shoulder and pulled her close. "But you're going to owe me, my friend. Big time."

"You name it. It's yours. What do you want in return?"

"Oh, no. That's not how this works. I'm not locking myself into anything. When it's time to collect, I'll let you know."

Maisie regarded me as if she were weighing a heavy decision. "But can I trust you not to take advantage of me...?"

"Definitely not." I shrugged as she laughed. "But

those are my stipulations. Take it or leave it. You want all this cleaned up and in a tux by tomorrow evening?" I ran a hand down my body and didn't miss the greedy look in her eyes as she followed it. "Then it's gonna cost you."

"You drive a hard bargain, Hutton. But, you have me by the balls here. Figuratively, of course. There's no way I'm heading back to that hotel without a best man in tow. You have no idea the level of Bridezilla that's awaiting us." Maisie linked arms with me again and headed toward the parking lot.

"Us?" I asked, as I stumbled along behind her.

"Damn straight, us. You think I'm just going to show back up without proof of acquisition?" She shook her head. "You obviously haven't met Brighton yet. Now come on, my friend." She gestured toward the parking lot. "Which one's yours?"

SEVEN

Maisie

CALEB SMELLED LIKE MAN, wrapped in ocean, and covered in sea salt. Not a combination I ever thought I'd appreciate, but appreciate it I did. He managed to make cargo shorts, a tank top, and flip flops look like Channing Tatum in a Magic Mike video— only with more muscles and sex appeal. He also had me wrapped around his little finger with that quiet confidence he discovered somewhere along the way as he grew.

Whatever he had in mind for calling in his favor— and my dirty little mind had a few...okay...*plenty* ideas of its own—then I might be willing to break several of my 'no strings attached' dating rules if it turned out we were thinking the same thing.

Caleb was sending very mixed signals and honestly, I was sure I was, too. Sometimes it felt like we were heading toward a hot hookup, but as soon as I started thinking it was inevitable, the mood would shift and he would start an obsessive round of calling me *friend*, almost like he was trying to brand the word on me somewhere.

He was into me, I could tell that much. But maybe our history was enough to weird him out. Or maybe he just wasn't *that* into me...cue a decade old movie to go with his decade old phone.

Either way, it felt wonderful to be with him again, especially when I came face to face with his choice of vehicle. "No way," I said, circling a retro convertible with a stellar blue and white paint job.

"You like?"

I leaned against the hood in what I hoped was my best pinup model pose. "Like it? I love it."

"She's a nineteen-fifty-six Ford Fairlane in peacock blue and colonial white. What she doesn't have in speed, she makes up for in style." Caleb grinned like a proud papa and I walked around the exterior, giving the car the attention it deserved. He followed me, then pulled open the passenger door and gestured for me to have a seat. "Milady," he said as he dropped into a surprisingly graceful bow.

"Why thank you, kind sir," I replied in my best British accent (hint: even my best wasn't very good) and I lowered myself into the soft, leather seat, groaning in appreciation as I ran my hand along the material.

He got the name of my hotel and brought the engine to life. Conversation flowed easily between us and I found myself growing more and more relieved to know he would be spending Brighton's wedding with me. As much as I appreciated my friends, Caleb's easy-going nature soothed a part of me I had forgotten existed. A part of me that hadn't gotten much playtime since I vowed to leave my Kentucky life behind.

He was just...happy. His life was what it was, the way he made it, and he seemed comfortable with his choices and with who he had become. Everything about him was out on display. Every truth. Every like. Every dislike. He didn't try to hide parts of himself the way everyone did in Los Angeles—myself included. His take-me-as-I-am-or-gtfo attitude was so refreshing, which was exactly why I didn't flinch even the slightest when Brighton gave him a hard onceover after she let us in her room.

"Not exactly digging the vibe here." She gestured

at his outfit and out-on-the-water-all-day hair. "Though something tells me he cleans up nice."

I slapped my friend on the shoulder. "Brighton! Not cool."

"Sorry." She gave me an apologetic look, then turned to Caleb. "I really am. Stress has eaten my soul. Forgive me?" She batted her eyelashes and put on her best I'm-really-quite-sweet face.

"Already forgiven," Caleb drawled, quite obviously playing up a southern accent he really didn't have and just like that, he had Brighton under his spell.

Well played, old friend. Well played.

They chatted about the specifics and Brighton thanked him roughly seven hundred times for stepping in during her hour of need. "I'll pay for the tuxedo rental, of course. It doesn't make sense for you to incur any cost while swooping in to rescue me."

"No worries. I have one of my own, though I'm not sure it'll work if you're doing some matchy-matchy color thing." Caleb gave me a look like a drowning man begging for help. Brighton's energy could be overbearing on her best days, and as she had already admitted, this was not one of those days.

She turned to me. "This guy just happens to have a tuxedo hanging in his closet, ready to go. Are you Bruce Wayne?" She leaned in to study his face. "You're Bruce Wayne, aren't you?" Her voice trailed off before she finished her joke, as she started really putting the pieces of his face together. "Oh my gosh! Maisie!" She turned back to me, gesturing wildly at the man standing between us. "He's your picture frame boy!"

Caleb gave me a wide-eyed look. "Picture frame boy?" he mouthed.

"Wow." Brighton stared at him, practically drooling. "Really...*wow*. You sure have filled out, haven't you?" She clutched one meaty bicep and gave it a squeeze. "I mean, who in their right mind would have thought that skinny little kid would turn into something like this?"

"Brighton! That. Is. Enough." I turned to Caleb, ready to apologize and die a hundred deaths of shame, but he gave an easy laugh.

"Certainly not that skinny little kid. Now," he said as he wrapped an arm around Brighton's shoulder and pulled her close. "Tell me about this picture."

EIGHT

Maisie

CALEB COULD WEAR the hell out of a tux. His tousled blonde hair was gelled to perfection. Broad shoulders seemed even broader thanks to the fantastic cut of the jacket. No one in Brighton's wedding party could take their eyes off him, men and women alike. I watched with a certain amount of pride as he fit in with this crowd of strangers like he had known them for years instead of just under an hour. His easy nature, his infectious smile, and that damn fake southern drawl had everyone charmed.

Me included.

The question in my mind was whether or not he knew he was doing it. After we left Brighton's hotel room yesterday, he had owned up to adopting the accent because he got a kick out of watching tourists swoon, but was the rest of his personality just as calculated? Or was he genuinely so laid back? He was like anti-anxiety pills personified. The human equivalent of medical marijuana. (Not that I was ever one to partake.) If Mrs. Hutton admitted to having a torrid love affair with Matthew McConaughey, with Caleb being the only evidence of the union, I would buy that story without flinching—even knowing Rebecca Hutton as well as I did when I was younger.

Brighton chose a tropical garden with an impeccably restored mansion on the property for the wedding and reception. Guests chattered in their seats as music filtered from hidden speakers and peacocks strutted around the scene. I stood with Caleb and the rest of the wedding party at the start of a long, white stretch of carpet that would lead us to our places before the happy couple said their vows. My bridesmaid dress was my favorite shade of blue, somehow managing to match the peacock feathers and knowing Brighton as well as I did, that was no coincidence. Too bad she and Sawyer wouldn't be driving away in Caleb's car, as it would truly be the perfect touch.

As the music swelled, I turned to the man who used to be my best friend. The man who still felt as comfortable and genuine as he did when we were kids.

The man whose eyes met mine and sent a shiver of desire humming along my spine. "You always did say we'd walk down the aisle together," I said, offering him my arm.

There. Hide behind humor. Great diversion tactic.

Caleb gave me a look I couldn't decipher. "Not exactly what I had in mind. But, beggars and choosers, you know?" He leaned in. "And I'd beg for you any day."

His words set off an explosion of butterflies in my stomach and I almost laughed out loud. Butterflies? *Butterflies?* I was immune to butterflies. I was an impenetrable fortress of butterfly resistance. I was...

Caleb placed his hand on the small of my back. "Come on, beautiful. Let's do this."

...totally swarmed with butterflies.

The music swelled and my heart was full as together, Caleb and I walked down the aisle, rows and rows of people smiling as we passed. How many times had he told me he was going to marry me when we were kids? How many times had I clung to those words like a lifeline? Caleb had been my anchor. My armor. He had been the one I turned to when I needed help and back then, I had been the only one he felt comfortable opening up to.

And now, all these years later, here we were, walking arm and arm past a sea of strangers, under a luscious canopy of tropical trees, keeping company with strutting peacocks elegantly fanning their feathers. If Sawyer heard this little plot twist to our story, I'm sure it, too, would get his 'perfectly ironic' seal of approval. For a tiny, happy little moment, I let the little girl inside me imagine that this was the day Caleb had always promised me. But all too quickly, we arrived at the end of carpet and separated to make space for the rest of the wedding party to take their places as the bride and groom started their walk toward us.

The ceremony began and I did my best to shake off the strange feelings. My stay in Key West was nearly over and Caleb's life was here. Soon, we'd be back to living our separate lives on opposite sides of the country. Indulging in daydreams seemed dangerous and if walking down the aisle with Caleb was Karma's way of closing the loop on our friendship, then I would smile at the gift and do my best to be grateful for it. Only greedy little girls asked for more.

Though, as Caleb caught my eye and grinned while Brighton and Sawyer said 'I do,' the urge to be greedy swelled right along with my heart.

DAMN THAT TUXEDO.

Damn the open bar.

Damn the DJ for choosing a perfect mix of love songs.

And damn Caleb for keeping me on the dancefloor all night, my body pressed to his as his hands roamed my back. With his cheek to mine and his strong arms guiding me into swooping dips and spinning swirls— where the hell did he learn to dance like that anyway? —the swarm of butterflies had disintegrated into white hot desire coursing through my veins.

I liked him.

And I wanted him.

And his perfect lips brushed my ear every time he spoke and...

"Caleb?" I murmured, letting myself get carried away with the alcohol and the atmosphere. "Did you ever want to kiss me when we were kids?"

He laughed lightly. "All the time."

The next thing I wanted to say was right on the tip of my drunken tongue. *Kiss me, Caleb. Kiss me now while the music is right and the mood is perfect. Kiss me in front of all these strangers, sweeping me off my feet and taking back your place as the most important person in my life. Kiss me and prove that fate exists and life is kind.*

Those words caught in my throat, struggling and straining to break past a giant lump of logic reminding me that our lives were too separate for him to be anything but a fond memory. Sometimes, I listened to logic. I valued logic. It had its place and was a powerful trait in the right circumstances.

But I hadn't climbed out of the ashes of my parents' bad decisions because I listened to logic. I hadn't listened to the people telling me it was foolish to dream —that poor-as-dirt little girls grew into poor-as-dirt women. I didn't listen to people warning me that Los Angeles was a place built on the broken dreams of people willing to sell their soul to get what they wanted. That the success stories were a tiny percentage of the truth and more often than not, people failed hard in that land of sunshine, smog, and nose jobs.

It wasn't logic that had me taking a chance on Collin West, with his red hair and awkward disposition. In fact, there was nothing logical about the way I chose who I wanted to represent. I listened to my intuition. It whispered to me during meetings, guiding me out of terrible decisions masquerading as sure things and pointing out the hidden gems that would make my career. It was intuition that sent me to LA. It was intuition that called for me to take the job as an intern at Paradigm Shift Talent Agency. It was intuition that landed me my first chance to represent someone as a full-blown agent.

My life was about listening when that little whispering voice started talking. In that moment, wrapped in Caleb's arms and swaying to soft music in a beautiful tropical garden, my intuition wasn't whispering. It was yammering away, reminding me that each second I let pass would be one less second I had with my old friend who grew into the perfect man. We had been tossed together like this for a reason.

If I let myself back away from him because I was afraid, then I wouldn't be half the woman I thought I was.

"What about now?" I asked, shoving the words past the lump of logic in my throat. "Do you want to kiss me now?"

Caleb met my gaze, still swaying to the music, but guiding us toward the outer edge of the dancefloor. He nodded slowly, his eyes hooded with lust as they dropped to my lips. "That's all I've wanted since we ran into each other at the bar."

I smiled up at him, knowing I was drunk. Knowing he was, too. Knowing that it was both too early and too late for us to be anything but a bad decision. But my intuition told me it was time to stop thinking. That worrying was getting us nowhere and the two of us were supposed to *be* something.

Caleb pressed firm hands to my back, sliding one up to cup the back of my head, the rough skin on his hands sliding over my shoulders and sending shivers dancing deliciously down my spine. He smiled as he met my eyes, our lips so close I could feel the heat between us. He whispered my name, angling his mouth to meet mine...

"There you are!" Brighton's shrill voice was a bucket of ice water dropped on my head. I stepped away from Caleb, energy vibrating in the space between us, as if in that pure and perfect moment of our almost kiss, his cells had invaded mine and our souls would be forever entangled.

"Oh!" Brighton stared, a knowing smile tugging at her lips and lighting up her eyes. "Worst timing ever. Sorry. But it's time for your speech." She wrinkled her nose apologetically and lifted a shoulder before taking my hand and leading me away.

Caleb took my other hand and gave Brighton his most charming smile. "Give us a minute," he said to her while pulling me back into his arms. His lips pressed to mine and one hand cupped my cheek. He tasted like champagne and memories, and a tidal wave of want threatened to crush me as I gave in to him.

"When do you go back to LA?" he asked, then kissed me again without waiting for me to reply.

Reality brought another bucket of ice water down on me. I stopped kissing him, imagining myself drenched and dripping in the middle of the room, hair ruined and makeup running. "Tomorrow."

Pulling away just enough to meet my eyes, Caleb gave an imperceptible shake of his head. "No. Stay longer. I'll get you a room at The Hut."

He left no room for argument, kissing me again, stealing my breath and my body as his lips moved against mine. I nodded and he released me, though something told me we would never fully separate again.

Brighton stared, jaw dropped, eyes alight with mirth and merriment, then took my hand and led me away.

NINE

Caleb

THE DRIVE UP to The Hut used to be a tense one. The closer I got to my family's home—traveling north through the islands—the closer I got to the memories of Dad and the terrible things he used to say to us when he was drunk. My anxiety would rise, and this bitter rock would settle into my stomach.

It wasn't like that anymore.

Especially not today, with my perma-grin and the giddy little boy inside me chanting *you kissed Maisie* over and over and over.

Since Dad's passing, I almost looked forward to pulling up in front of our old house. The energy was lighter and brighter, especially after Wyatt had the office renovated and all of Dad's furniture removed. Mom was happier than I could remember her being in years. The kind of happy that had no ifs, ands, or buts behind it. Her eyes were bright and her smile was easy and I swore, she walked as if a weight had finally fallen from her shoulders.

The same could be said for all of us, really.

A shroud had been lifted off our family now that Dad was gone. My two older brothers were married and paraded around like the most satisfied men in the history of the world. While Lucas would always be intense and brooding, he was quick to laugh when he was around his wife, Cat. Wyatt had always been a bright spot in our family, the man who stepped into the patriarchal hole Dad left behind, but so much of that had been a show for our benefit. With all of Dad's craziness draining out of his system, the difference in Wyatt was noticeable. His marriage to Kara had turned up the colors in his life and looking back, I don't know how we missed how miserable he used to be. Now, his natural positivity truly knew no bounds.

I pulled to a stop in front of what had once been my family home, then grew to a bed and breakfast, and was now the main building of The Hutton Hotel. It was early still, the sun hanging low and bright over the water, sending explosions of color up to the sky. A breeze sent the palm fronds dancing and the ferns hanging along the wraparound porch swayed their welcome.

Once upon a time, I believed the welcoming exterior to be a lie, knowing that a monster hid inside. But the monster was gone and I finally saw what everyone else did. It was a beautiful place, this home of ours.

Mom pushed open the front door as I took the steps onto the porch. Her red braid hung over one shoulder and her smile fought the sunrise for splendor. "Is that my Caleb?" She held open her arms and I stepped into them. "I didn't expect to see you today," she said as she let me go.

"I had a couple things I wanted to talk about. You won't believe who I ran into the other night."

And *I* couldn't believe who I had kissed last night. After fighting the urge the entire evening, after a lifetime of turning down short-term relationships, after years of assuming I would never see her again, I finally kissed Maisie Brown.

The girl I always thought I would marry.

The girl who always had an inroad straight to the core of me.

The woman who was supposed to leave today—but chose to stay anyway.

I was walking on air while trying not to fall off the edge of a cliff. Thrilled and terrified and desperate to spend every second with her before we had no more seconds left.

"I cooked a big ole breakfast today," Mom said. "There's plenty for everyone, even you and your giant appetite. Come, grab a plate. You can tell me everything while we eat." She stopped, a quizzical frown tightening her brows. "Unless you need to talk in private?"

My stomach started grumbling at the mere mention of breakfast and I shook my head. "Nope. I don't need to say anything everyone can't hear."

Mom beamed and led me back to the kitchen, where our old family table sat, surrounded by windows, with the ocean stretching out behind them. The table was full, and everyone was there except my younger brother, Eli.

As I stepped into the room, Wyatt scooted his chair out and stood to wrap me in a hug, thumping me on the back before pulling away. "Well, look what the cat dragged in."

With a lot of commotion and a little rearranging, I found a spot next to my sister Harlow. A plate of eggs, biscuits, and bacon appeared in front of me, and I momentarily forgot why I made the drive to The Hut in the first place.

I listened, smiling, as my family chattered, Cat and Kara fitting in with the rest as if they had been part of the family for decades. That thought brought me back to Maisie, who actually *had* been an honorary Hutton for decades.

I put my fork down and cleared my throat. "I walked down the aisle with Maisie Brown last night."

That should be enough to shock them into silence.

It was. Momentarily. A few stunned seconds later, the questions started launching my way while I laughed.

"It's not as crazy as it sounds," I said. "Though, it's crazy enough."

Everyone listened as I explained Maisie's sudden appearance at the bar, her friend's dramatic need for a stand-in best man, and how much her life had changed for the better.

"Who's Maisie?" Cat whispered to Lucas when I was done with the story.

"Only Caleb's first and longest crush." Wyatt grinned like a lunatic and wrapped an arm around Kara's shoulder.

Harlow leaned forward, pushing her plate out of the way to make room for her elbows. "Maisie's the one you always swore you'd marry, right?"

The questions streamed my way and I fielded them like a pro. "Anyway," I said when the excitement died down, "she was supposed to leave today, but I talked her into hanging around a little longer. She needs a place to stay and I thought you guys might like a chance to see her again, so I offered her a room here."

I had been right about the energy of my family changing. Instead of tight sighs and furrowed brows, perhaps a glance toward the office where Dad would be lurking to drop in on the conversation with complaints about reservations and ridiculous chance meetings with childhood friends, my family smiled in unison.

Heads started nodding. Eyes gleamed. In a matter of seconds, Maisie had a bungalow reserved for as long as she planned on staying.

The front door opened and closed and footsteps sounded in the entry. Wyatt pushed to his feet, wiped his mouth, and then bounded out to greet whoever had walked in, only to return a few seconds later with a grinning Maisie tucked under his arm.

TEN

Maisie

THE DRIVE UP from Key West was...unusual. My boss seemed to think he could force me back to Los Angeles with a sheer abundance of foul language and veiled threats. He was wrong.

I wasn't coming back to LA. Not yet.

I had earned time off. I was taking it. The end.

After ending the call, realization settled uncomfortably onto my shoulders. Yes, I was on my way to see Caleb and his family, but I was also heading back to my childhood stomping grounds—a place I swore I would never set foot in again. Rare buds of anxiety bloomed in my stomach, more and more of them blossoming into existence the closer I got to the turn off that would take me to the shack I once called home. With effort, I turned my attention to Caleb and The Hut. To the soul-melting kiss we shared at the wedding and his insistence that I stay in the Keys.

There were so many unanswered questions...

How long would I be here?

How far would this go?

What did I think was going to happen?

What about when it all came to an end?

Those questions were born of logic and fear and I wasn't ready to give them any weight yet. Caleb felt important. He felt real. And if I had to bury my head in the sand for a little bit to enjoy this monumental gift, then so be it.

We would deal with the logistical stuff when we got there. Now was the time to focus on what we had, not what was at stake. Who knew how this would play out?

Maybe this was nothing more than a great day or two of pure physical attraction.

Maybe last night's kiss would lead to some of the best sex of our lives.

Or...

Maybe we could reignite our old friendship.

Maybe Caleb would move to Los Angeles and make good on his old childhood promise.

The future was uncertain, nothing more than infinite possibilities stretching out in front of us. I'd be a fool to hold back just because some of those possibilities were a little scary. Because the rest? They were magnificent.

I grinned as I pulled into the lot at The Hut, right next to the work of art Caleb called a vehicle. This place was the home of so many happy memories. Rebecca Hutton's warm smile. The siblings welcoming me as if I was one of them. Longs days with Caleb near the water, him fishing and me just dangling my legs off the dock and thinking big thoughts. Back then, the Huttons always laughed so easily, so deeply, it made me uncomfortable. Back then, I wasn't used to being secure enough to laugh.

I ran my hand up the rail as I stepped up to the porch, lost in the memories of younger me racing Caleb outside, my hair streaming behind me, our arms and legs pumping as fast as they could. Potted ferns swung lazily in the breeze and I remembered perching on the edge of an Adirondack chair, clutching a glass of lemonade and slurping it down while sweat beaded at my temples and Caleb chattered away about our next greatest adventure.

A sign near the door said "come on in" so I did just that, quietly closing the door behind me. The entryway looked exactly as I remembered it, though the office had changed significantly. When I was little, Mr. Hutton's office was a place of sullen shadows and looming furniture, but now, the windows were open and sunlight warmed the room. A vibrant painting adorned the wall over a simple desk, while plants and flowers brightened the space. No more looming shadows. No more hints of whispered secrets. Just happy, welcoming energy. Somehow, that particular change put my heart at ease.

Movement caught my attention and I glanced up to find a man emerging from the kitchen. He was tall, but not as tall as Caleb, blond-haired and blue-eyed enough to let me know I was looking at a Hutton. He grinned when he saw me, a vibrant smile that lit up the whole room, and I knew immediately which brother was in front of me.

Wyatt crossed the room and wrapped me in a tight hug. "Caleb was just telling us about you."

In a swoop of energy, he ushered me into the kitchen. The family greeted me like there wasn't a decade separating us, and introduced me to Cat and Kara, Lucas and Wyatt's wives.

Caleb beamed when he saw me, standing to offer me his chair, as his good-natured eyes drank me in. If I had been afraid that his invitation to stay had anything to do with the alcohol or the atmosphere last night—

and let me admit, those thoughts had popped into my head a time or two—the fear dissipated the moment he touched me. "Hey there," he said, his gaze dropping to my mouth.

"Hey yourself." I licked my lips and fought the urge to kiss him in front of most of his family. I didn't know how much Caleb had told them about what was going on and certainly didn't want to spill the beans on...on...whatever this was between us.

Before I could take the chair he offered me, Rebecca was out of hers and making her way to me. She gripped my shoulders and held me at arm's length, studying all the changes growing up had brought to my face. "Maisie Brown," she said, her voice lilting like a proud momma. "Just look at you! I always knew you'd be beautiful, but..." She shook her head, then pulled me in for a hug. "I'm just happy to see you looking so...so..."

"Clean?" I offered, returning the hug.

"I was going to say polished," Rebecca replied. "Looks like you've done very well for yourself."

In a matter of seconds, I found myself seated next to Caleb with a plate of breakfast food in front of me that would have Brighton running in fear from all the fat and carbs. Normally, I took my breakfast in the form of caffeine and optimism, but everything smelled so delicious, I explained my new life around mouthfuls of biscuits, gravy, and bacon. "Oh my goodness," I said to Rebecca. "This is so good."

The family listened incredulously as I outlined my story. They asked about my parents and I gave them the short and simple answer: nothing much had changed. They were still locked in a cruel cycle of getting jobs, losing jobs, and Dad drinking away their savings. "I send them money each month, but honestly, I'm conflicted about it. I know they need it, but I'm afraid they don't use it for anything good."

Those two sentences were the first time I had spoken to anyone about my parents since I moved out of their house. And here I was, within minutes of arriving at The Hut, talking openly about the parts of my life I intended to keep buried forever. I wasn't even sure I recognized how conflicted I was about the money I sent their way until I spoke. The realization dumbfounded me, and I shoved another bite of biscuit into my mouth before I could say anything else.

The conversation moved on as the family filled me in on their lives. I learned about Lucas' tragedy in Afghanistan and the jaw-dropping set of coincidences that led him to meet his wife. Wyatt introduced me to Kara, and their story had me on the edge of my seat. Harlow explained that she had been living in Seattle, painting, playing guitar, and working on a novel when Mr. Hutton had passed away.

"I think I'm here to stay though," she said, tossing her long, blonde hair over a shoulder. "Maybe I can finally finish my book and see about finding a publisher."

"And what about Eli?" I asked. "Things good with him?"

Harlow grinned. "Eli's Eli. Doing his own thing and making his own way."

Time passed easily as we reminisced. Stories flowed and the truth of my past was out in the open for the first time in a decade. In LA, no one could know that poor-as-dirt little girl was me and I was her. But here, with the Huttons, it just was a truth that everyone knew and everyone accepted. There was a comfort in that, as well as a heavy dose of unease. I didn't want to be her anymore. For some reason, acknowledging that we were one and the same felt like I was doing the new me a disservice. It almost felt like moving backwards.

"Remember that?" Wyatt leaned in, laughing so hard I could barely understand him. "Dad had questions about Caleb's sexual orientation for a year."

"Wait. What?" I tried to mentally replay the conversation to catch up to everyone else.

"When we walked in and found you two playing

with makeup..." Wyatt lost himself to giggles as Kara stared at Caleb with astounded eyes.

"Come on now." Caleb sat back in his chair, running his hands through his hair. "We were, what? Seven? Eight?" He looked to me for support. "And I looked damn good in that mascara."

Cat shook her head and leaned forward, her voice filled with merriment. "I'm just trying to imagine our Moose wearing makeup."

"I did it for her, okay?" Caleb wrapped an arm around my shoulder and drew me close. "That's just the kind of friend I am."

We turned to each other, pleased with the memory, and when our eyes met, a jolt of electricity bounced through me, trailing along my skin, lighting up my insides. I was sure everyone could see it. Hell, I was sure everyone could *feel* it. The attraction between us leaping out from where our eyes locked, to the long line of contact where his arm connected with my shoulders, and dancing along the table, like lightening arcing from cloud to cloud.

Someone coughed and someone else cleared a throat and Caleb dropped his arm from my shoulder like we had been caught doing something equally ridiculous as me putting makeup on him. Now that he wasn't touching me, it was easier to breathe and I hoped no one caught the chemistry oozing between us.

One glance around the table told me everything I needed to know.

Oozing chemistry had very much been caught.

"Well," Wyatt said, his eyes twinkling devilishly. "I guess there's no questioning his sexual orientation now."

ELEVEN

Caleb

AS IF ON CUE, my family gathered their plates from the table and excused themselves to begin their work day, leaving Maisie and me with nothing but the charged atmosphere to keep us company. She shook her head at Wyatt's statement, a slight blush bringing color to her cheeks and I could have sworn she looked pleased about what he said.

I liked that she wanted me to want her. I liked that she wasn't bothered that the attraction was obvious. I liked that we were still amazing together, even after she had grown up in such an unforeseen way.

I wanted to draw her into my arms and hold her close, to press my lips to hers, to unwrap her like the gift she was and claim her as mine, but if last night was any indicator, there would be no stopping once we started. The family kitchen seemed like the worst place to start something like that, so I settled back in my chair and regarded Maisie from a distance. "Having second thoughts about staying yet?"

She sighed dramatically, bobbing her head as her supple lips pulled into a grimace. "Totally. I didn't know how to let you down easy, so I thought I'd wait until *after* your whole family had a chance to see whatever that was that just happened between us." She lifted a playful brow, but I wasn't buying it.

"Uh-huh..."

"No, silly." Maisie folded her arms on the table and leaned in. "No second thoughts. They're not really my style. Once a ball is in play, it's best to let it roll and see what happens."

I couldn't help myself. She set the line up so perfectly, I would be letting the entire world down if I didn't take the shot. "So...you're saying you want to play with my balls."

I didn't know what I expected of her. Maybe a blush. Maybe a shy little giggle. I hoped I wouldn't get shocked silence and a slow back-peddle out the door.

I *did* know the last thing I expected from sweet little Maisie was a wry smile and the words, "If you're lucky," followed by a burst of laughter when my jaw dropped.

"Don't look so shocked, Hutton. This is me and you we're talking about. No barriers. Remember?"

"Right. No barriers. Except half our life and the entire country."

Maisie stood and pushed in her chair. "Right. Except that." Questions filled her eyes as they bounced across my face, and for a moment, the bold, brash, LA Maisie was gone. In her place stood someone who looked vulnerable and sad and unsure. But then she blinked and smiled and I wondered if maybe my imagination was getting the better of me.

"So now what?" she asked. "Do I need to check in? Put a credit card on file? Sign my name in blood? I've heard it's hard to get a room here."

I stood, then leaned on the back of the chair. "Nope. Everything's already taken care of and you absolutely won't be paying. It's yours for as long as you'll be here."

The next question was obvious. *How long will you be here, anyway?* But I pushed it away like a child humming with his fingers in his ears. I wanted to revel in her company and ignore her impending departure

"Tomorrow I'm pretty jampacked with tours, but my schedule is wide open today. I'm all yours. Interested in going out on the water? I know a place."

"A place, huh? What kind of place?"

"A cove a few miles out. It's beautiful. And secluded. And, the last time I took my family there, I'm pretty sure Cat fell in love with Lucas, so you know, it's not my fault if you fall in love with me." I held up my hands. "Just sayin.'"

Maisie laughed lightly. "Nothing to worry about there. I've been in love with you since we were six years old."

She was joking. I knew it. It was clear through the lilt in her voice and the twinkle in her eyes, but her words hit me harder than that kid in seventh grade. I did my best not to let her see it as we got her luggage from her car and I escorted her to her bungalow. I chatted happily, as if her words meant nothing to me. And really, they shouldn't have meant anything. Sure, I spent years six through thirteen of my life swearing I would marry her. But years fourteen through twenty-six made me see how silly I had been to believe that.

Maisie was nothing but a childhood fantasy.

The product of a little kid's romantic streak. A kid that didn't understand how much life could change in the blink of an eye.

She was also one hell of a woman, whose soft hair kept brushing my shoulder as she leaned into me on our way to her room.

I swung open the door to her bungalow with a flourish. "Welcome home, beautiful."

Maisie's eyes bulged and her jaw dropped as she took in the tastefully decorated space with a four-poster bed, luxurious tub, and a walk-out patio with a private ocean view. "I knew the hotel had grown since we were little, but wow! Look at this place!" She darted around the room, checking out the amenities, *ooh*'ing and *ahh*'ing over the fabric and color choices. She flopped onto the bed with a sigh, then rolled onto her side, rubbing an appreciative hand over the comforter. "It's so soft. And inviting. I'm not sure I'll ever want to leave."

The innuendo settled over us like the heavy scent of perfume, invisible, yet impossible to ignore.

"Good." I smiled at her. "Don't." Before she could respond, I hurried on because it was either get the hell out of there or join her on that bed and ravish her on the spot. "There's a few things I need to get ready down at the dock, so how about you take some time to get settled in and then meet me at the boat at one?"

Seduction was an art. There was something powerful about the slow build of want and need. Waiting until the electricity between us climbed to a fevered pitch so that the sparks exploded into full on wildfire when we finally came together.

The cove was a perfect space to stoke the embers

growing between us. To learn more about who she was and what she wanted and then, with the quiet lap of water against the boat and the stars glittering to life in the darkening sky, move in to show her just how much it meant to me that she stayed when she was supposed to leave.

Maisie nodded her agreement and I beelined out of there before all the dirty thoughts in my head took control and my 'art of seduction' looked more like a Kindergartner with a crayon than Picasso with a paintbrush.

Maisie

BY THE TIME I made my way down to the docks, I had answered approximately one million emails and texts from people less than thrilled about my extended stay in the Keys. When they found out said extended stay didn't exactly have an expiration date? Yeah. There were a lot of people very angry with Maisie Brown.

It wasn't like me to bail on work responsibilities and I already felt guilty about it *before* sending what felt like several hundred apologies to irate clients and co-workers. I did get one very sweet text from Brighton, congratulating me on my decision to stay with 'picture frame boy' and wishing me well on my sex-cation. I still wasn't sure that was where Caleb and I were headed, especially after I did everything but rip off my clothes and drop down on my knees in my room and he didn't take the bait.

You're overanalyzing and that never works out well for you. Stop it. Go with the flow. Follow your instincts. They haven't let you down yet.

I bobbed my head as I talked myself back from the edge of anxiety. Nothing about my life turned out the way I planned it, yet it had worked out to be amazing anyway. Worrying too much about how something was supposed to happen almost always resulted in a frustrated Maisie with less than stellar results. When I relaxed enough to let go and trust the process, things always fell into place.

The sun shone down, glinting off the sand as my sandals kicked up dust behind me. I could see Caleb, shirt off, sweat gleaming on his tanned skin, muscles flexing as he worked the ropes and readied the boat for our little adventure. The closer I got to him, the more the guilt over missing work faded. I had dedicated my life to the people at Shift. This was a rare moment for myself and there was no reason to feel bad about being a little self-centered. Self-care was important. Especially when it came in the form of Caleb Hutton.

He glanced up and saw me making my way onto the dock, a grin sliding across his face as he lifted a hand in greeting. "Hey there, beautiful," he drawled in that oh-so-sexy but oh-so-fake southern accent of his.

"Hey yourself," I said as I took the hand he offered and stepped onto the boat.

He worked with a laid-back precision defined the man he had become. Confident and smooth. Easygoing, but exacting. Being around him made me relax enough to forget my phone that I buried in my bag and the onslaught of messages that had certainly come in since the last time I checked. The wind moved through my hair and I allowed myself to sit back and do nothing but watch Caleb in his element as he navigated us through the water into a cove that was truly breathtaking.

"Oh, wow," I breathed as the boat slowed to a stop. Clear water glittered in the sunlight. Palm trees dotted a secluded beach. "It's perfect." I turned to Caleb, whose gaze was locked on my smiling face.

"It really is," he replied, and I got the distinct impression he wasn't talking about the view.

TWELVE

Maisie

WE SWAM FOR A WHILE, diving right off the boat into the cool water. Then we lounged for a while, salt drying on our skin as we baked in the sun. We talked about all the things. Our hopes. Our dreams. Our memories. The time we spent together as kids and all the silly games we used to play. The strange paths life opened for us, that led us right back here to each other.

"You know," I said, leaning back in my seat and closing my eyes. "I never really saw myself becoming a talent agent. I always saw myself helping people... thanks to you and your influence on my life. You helped me so much, protecting me, feeding me, making me feel like I belonged to something bigger than myself. I wanted to pass that feeling on to as many people as I could. But an agent?" I gave a little shrug of my shoulders. "I'm just as surprised as anyone that this is where I ended up."

Caleb draped an arm over his seat and crossed his ankle over his knee. "If I'm being honest, LA is the last place I would have imagined you."

I bobbed my head. "Yeah. Me too. But I'm happy there. I *am* helping people, even if it's not the way I always assumed I would. It's a very fulfilling life."

I had said those words so many times in the last few years. *It's a very fulfilling life.* Each time I said them—including today—I meant them with all of me. I had nothing but gratitude for the opportunities that had opened for me. For the chance encounters and strange coincidences that led me to where I was. For all the hard work through high school and college that built up a reservoir of strength that helped me weather the demands my clients made each day.

This time though, the words seemed oddly hollow. Maybe it was the slew of angry messages from earlier. The sense that for all I was willing to sacrifice for other people, the second I wanted something for myself, they were offended by the choice.

I brushed those thoughts away. It *was* selfish of me to take more time off without planning for it first. My decisions didn't just affect me. They rippled down through all the lives I touched. People had every right to be exasperated with me and I would make this it all up to them as soon as I could.

"That's all that matters then, isn't it?" Caleb asked. "Living a fulfilling life. What's the point of it all if we can't spend each day happy?"

Images of my parents, of the friends I met in Kentucky, of the people I worked with in LA popped into my head—all of them with stress humming along underneath the surface of their skin, a toxic blend of cortisol, adrenaline, and caffeine rocketing through their veins. "That's a bit of a high bar, don't you think?"

Caleb looked genuinely confused. "What? Expecting to enjoy life? I'd say that's a low bar if you ask me."

"The vast majority of people in the world would disagree with you." I thought of the desperation I saw in the clients of Paradigm Shift Talent Agency. Those still waiting for their break were ready to do just about anything to get there. Those who had already gotten their were terrified they would fall from grace at any minute. Even living the dream didn't guarantee happiness.

And our clients? They were the lucky ones. So many people struggled day in and day out. My family was a prime example. *His* family was a prime example

—though their issues weren't financial. I said as much and Caleb sighed.

"That's the thing, though. Everyone is out chasing happiness like it's a destination and I feel like we've all been sold a great big lie. Real happiness is accepting who we are, where we are, and knowing we're being true to ourselves. Achievement. Money. Success. Those are false measures."

"That's easy to say for a person who came from money." It didn't even occur to me to censor myself until after the words were out of my mouth. Maybe LA had made me too bold. Maybe success had me thinking I could say anything and get away with it. Or maybe being with Caleb felt so natural, I didn't have to be anyone but who I was. Whatever the reason, I probably could have said that with more grace and braced myself for his reaction.

"Maybe." Caleb shrugged easily, not at all offended by my directness. "Though as soon as I was eighteen, I moved out of The Hut—and I hadn't even graduated high school yet. Supported myself on a fast food salary until I could open up my business. Lived in an apartment with a terrible roommate and very little furniture. I made every financial mistake in the book, but I wouldn't accept one single cent of support from my family because I wanted nothing to do with my father. While I have money now, and I had money as a kid, I do know what it's like to want things you can't have. To need things you can't buy. I've done my fair share of worrying where my next meal would come from."

This was the first I'd heard of this chapter in Caleb's story and I leaned forward, inviting him to continue.

"My dad was a bad man, May-belle." He offered a wry smile. "I wanted nothing to do with his lifestyle, so I created my own. My choices weren't without hardships, but I learned early on what it was that made life seem easy and I just kept iterating until I found myself where I am now."

"And where are you now?"

"Happy."

I stared at him long and hard, trying to read between the lines, to hear the things he wasn't saying and see if I got a sense that his story was as fake as that southern drawl of his. I found nothing.

Caleb gestured at the cove, the broad sweep of his arm taking in the water, the sky, the sun, and the sand. "I spend my days outside, enjoying the laughter of people around me, surrounded by some of the most beautiful scenery on the planet. How could I not be happy?"

The man had a point, and his confidence dazzled me. "And there isn't anything that you want? Not one thing that has you thinking 'if only I had this, my life would be complete?'"

Caleb gave me a smile that would charm the bikini off any tourist. "Well, there is one thing."

He stood and held out his hand. I placed mine in his and he pulled me up, wrapping me in his arms and gently swaying to the rhythm of the waves. "I was going to wait until the sun set and the stars came out," he said. "When the atmosphere was better suited for slow-dancing and honesty. But yes, there is one thing I want." He ran a thumb along my cheek, one hand pressed into my lower back.

I draped my arms around his shoulders, swaying in time to his slow movements, falling into his bottomless blue eyes. "And just what might that be?"

Caleb pressed his cheek against mine. "See, there was this girl I used to know." His words whispered in my hair and his lips brushed my ear. "And she was the best thing that ever happened to me." He kissed the delicate skin on my neck, just below my jaw. "But she was taken from me before I ever got to see if I was being a foolish romantic or not."

I tilted my head, allowing him better access to my throat as goosebumps flared to life down my spine. "Sounds like a cruel twist of fate to me."

"Oh, it was." He ran his hands along my waist. "So unbelievably cruel."

"So, what is it you want?" I pulled back to meet his devastatingly handsome face. "What is that one thing that would make your life complete?"

"In this moment? Nothing more than a kiss." And with that, he pressed his lips against mine, his strong arms supporting me as I opened to him. My tongue darted out to meet his as the molten heat of desire surged to life in my core.

"And what about now?" I asked, my lips brushing his. "Now that you've had your kiss?"

"Now, I just want the girl." He cupped the back of my head, angling his mouth over mine, fully encompassing me. One hand grabbed my butt and I wrapped my legs around his waist. Caleb took my weight with ease and I moaned into his mouth, just in time for the sound of my phone to catch my attention.

I stiffened with the instant urge to answer and the ingrained fear that I was missing something important that would fall to pieces if I didn't deal with it in that very moment. But in that moment, he was the only thing worth my time and I gave myself to him, returning his kiss with heat and passion. He lowered himself to his knees, depositing me on a chair and spreading my legs with his body as he cupped my face between his strong hands.

My phone buzzed again and this time, he paused. "Do you need to get that?"

I shook my head and kissed him again, even as the heat between us cooled. My phone buzzed again. Then again. I closed my eyes. "I'm sorry," I said, wishing I'd thought to put the thing on silent.

Caleb ran a thumb over my bottom lip. "Don't even worry about it. Just consider that a hint at what's to come."

I scrambled out of the seat and dug into my bag for my phone, cursing as I saw my boss' name on the caller ID. "I'm so sorry..." I began before accepting the call and turning away as I put the phone to my ear.

THIRTEEN

Caleb

MAISIE'S entire demeanor changed the moment she answered her call. Tension seethed from her posture as she paced the small deck. She rubbed her forehead as her words rat-a-tat-tatted into the phone, then pinched the bridge of her nose as she spoke in a tight voice.

"Look, I don't care what he said—" She paused as whoever was on the other end interrupted her. "Yeah, well, West's an ass. A talented ass, but an ass nonetheless. You can't—"

Another unfinished sentence and a long sigh as she held the phone away from her ear and flipped the screen the bird. All the happiness left her face, leaving nothing but the grit and determination that had gotten her to where she was. It didn't look pleasant. Not at all. It looked like she was gearing up for a fistfight. Like lives hung in the balance. Like maybe, all the talk about her fabulous life was covering up some not so wonderful truths.

To me, the Los Angeles fame scene had always seemed like a place for cutthroats who were willing to do anything to get what they wanted. Surely, the assessment was unfair. Afterall, I had never been there to see for myself. But the sudden shift in Maisie's demeanor wasn't doing anything to change the way I saw that city. It wasn't where dreamers went to be discovered. It was where souls went to die.

She finished her call with a low growl and her fingers clicked furiously on the screen as she sent several messages, muttering to herself the entire time. Her face was a mess of frustration as she chewed on the inside of her lip and scowled. Finally, she tossed her phone into her bag. Took a moment to run her hands through her hair and gather it over her shoulder before turning to me.

"I'm really sorry about that," she said, smiling like she hadn't just stepped out of an anger tornado. "It's kind of what I get for taking time off at the last second like this." She sauntered my way, her smile saying one thing—*I'm all yours, Moose*—and her eyes saying another—*I'm still pissed about that call*. "Now, where were we?"

I held out my hands, inviting her into my lap. "I think we were somewhere along right here," I said before taking one soft, supple lip between my teeth then releasing it to kiss her deeply, hoping I could soothe her frazzled soul with tenderness and undivided attention.

For as much as I tried to reclaim the heat of the moment, Maisie seemed a million miles away. Finally, she pressed her forehead to mine. "I really am sorry..." she began again but didn't finish the sentence. I couldn't tell if she was sorry for answering the call, for being distracted by whatever was happening, or for her life in general.

"Feel like talking about it?"

Maisie shook her head. "Nah." She pushed off my lap and leaned on the edge of the boat, staring out at the water. A heavy wind blew in off the ocean, the chill in the air alerting me to a change in the weather. Her phone kept buzzing like a pissed off little hornet and the weight on her shoulders grew with each missed text or call.

"Is it always like this?" I asked.

She let out a short little laugh. "This is an easy day." She shook herself visibly. "That's not true. Some days are difficult. You know, the cliché of the temperamental artist exists for a reason." She offered a bright smile that I was starting to think was a piece of armor instead of a genuine expression. "But sometimes we win big. You know? Like when I land that huge deal for an artist or negotiate that bigger payout." She bobbed her head as if she were trying to sell herself on a story she wasn't quite aware she was selling.

"But even then, it's missing something isn't it?"

Maisie frowned, two deep lines etched between her brows. "Sometimes even the successes feel really hollow. Like this guy I'm working for now. He's so talented. He has more potential in his pinky finger than some people have in their entire body. And at first, it felt like I had found this light to shine onto the world. Turns out he's *such* an egotistical prick..." Maisie sighed and shook herself again. "But if all I ever did was focus on the negative side of this business, I wouldn't be where I am. Things are better for me than I ever dreamed possible."

She was lying to herself. I could see it clear as day. She had all the flash and glamor she never had as a kid —which had to feel like a win—but it wasn't feeding her soul. She was missing something and didn't even know it.

Her phone buzzed again and her head dropped just as the low rumble of thunder sounded in the distance. "Tell you what," I said. "You answer that and put out whatever fires are burning back home. I'll get us back to The Hut before that storm hits and we'll pick up where we left off later." I ran a hand through her hair and met those soulful blue eyes.

My instinct was to throw her phone into the water. To rescue her from the bully just like I used to when we were younger. But we weren't kids anymore and Maisie could take care of herself.

At least that's what I kept telling myself as she dug through her bag, carrying more weight on those slim shoulders than seemed humanly possible.

FOURTEEN

Maisie

THE TRIP back to The Hut was both choppy and nauseating. The growing storm had the waves increasing in strength and the temper tantrum Collin had thrown when he saw the size of his part in the movie I negotiated for him had my stomach churning. I mean, I don't know how much more clear I could have been. A bit part was small by definition. It was also one hell of start for a musician who just hit the scene. His lack of gratitude made me angry. I called in half a dozen favors and worked a miracle for him, and he threw a fit because it wasn't big enough.

But more than the anger and frustration, more than the nausea, embarrassment boiled through my body.

I was embarrassed that Caleb saw me barking orders at my personal assistant—as if she had anything to do with what happened. Embarrassed that he saw my boss tear into me like I was a poorly behaved dog. Embarrassed that he saw the ugly underbelly of my perfect little life. He seemed so happy. So content. So aware of what it was he wanted and needed. When I answered that phone, it became clear he and I didn't operate on the same level.

Yes, I busted my butt to make other people's lives better, and yes, sometimes the payout was amazing, but more often than not, my lifestyle took a toll. I had always assumed that was the price I paid for success, but Caleb brought joy to people as well and if he paid for it, I sure as hell couldn't tell. What could possibly happen in his life that would have him yelling into his phone the way I just did? Hell, he didn't even have a smartphone. I didn't think you could *be* mad while holding a flip phone to your ear.

We made it back to the dock just as the sky unleashed a holy fury on us. The raindrops fell fast and hard, stinging when they slapped against my skin, and my hair was matted to my head in seconds. I shoved my phone deep into my bag so the rain wouldn't hurt it even when part of me wanted to throw it in the ocean and be done with everyone it connected me to.

"What can I do?" I yelled over the wind as Caleb sprang into action, securing the boat.

He pulled me into his arms and kissed me. The rain ran down our faces. I tasted the elements on his skin and lightening flashed in the distance. "Just that," he said, then kissed me again. "And that." Another kiss. "And that." He drew back, smiling as he blinked the rain out of his thick lashes. "Now, get inside and dry off. I've got this."

I tried to argue, but he wouldn't hear it. Before I knew what was happening, I was back in the privacy of my bungalow, drying my face and stripping out of my wet clothes in between answering texts. Collin's tantrum had escalated and now I had not only him to deal with, but also the studio, his label, and my boss' boss all acting like they had the solution to the problem. (Pro-tip: There wasn't a problem. Collin had speaking lines in a movie during his first year of stardom. There were musicians who went their entire career and never made it onto the silver screen.)

I washed my face, then pulled on a pair of sweatpants and a tank top, piling my hair into a messy bun on top of my head. Intending to get to work, I grabbed my laptop and sat on the bed, but my mind spun circles around Caleb.

Was he angry with me for cutting our day short?

(Probably not. The storm was going to do that for us anyway.)

Did he understand? (Probably. This was Caleb, after all.)

When could I see him again? (As soon as possible, please!)

If it was that explosive when we kissed, what would happen when we finally had sex? (I didn't have an answer for that one, but trying to come up with one was...interesting.)

Would we finally have sex? (If I have any say in the matter, then yes. Definitely.)

Or, was it foolishness for me to still be in the Keys at all? (No. I meant yes. I meant...)

"Damn it, Maisie," I muttered, flopping onto my back. I stared at the ceiling as my stomach growled, reminding me that I hadn't eaten since breakfast, and I had no idea what time it was. "Enough with the over-analyzing already."

My phone buzzed just as a knock scared the hell out of me. I answered the call, pinching the device between my ear and my shoulder as I moved to open the door and found a smiling Caleb standing there with a bag of carryout in his hands.

"I'll call you right back," I said to Collin, then hung up before he could respond.

"Ballsy." Caleb lifted an eyebrow. "I like it." The

sun hung low in the sky, setting it ablaze in a symphony of color. For the first time since I made it back to my room, I became aware of the rhythmic rush of the waves. What else had I missed while I hustled like hell to soothe Collin West's temperamental soul?

Caleb held up the bag of food. "I had the kitchen make you some dinner."

"You didn't have to do that," I said as I took it from him, greedily peering at the stacks of containers inside.

"Yes, I did." He leaned against the doorframe and shoved his hands in his pockets, giving me the most charming smile I had ever seen. (And I came from the land of handsome men and perfect smiles, so that was saying something.) "I got the impression you wouldn't have remembered to feed yourself until too late."

He was right. It happened all too often. I'd look up from one of the many screens in front of me and realize it was too late to worry about food. "Oh, yeah?" I asked, curious to see how he'd respond. "What makes you say that?"

"You take care of everyone else's needs over your own."

"That's not true." Taking care of everyone else's needs *was* taking care of my needs. That was how I paid my debt to the universe at large, for handing me the tools I needed to dig my way out of my parents' life.

"Really?" Caleb cocked his head and drew his eyebrows together. "What time is it, May-bell?"

I had no clue and he knew it. Laughing, I checked my phone, and there was no hiding the surprise on my face when I saw it was eight o'clock.

My stomach rumbled its gratitude for the food in my hand just as another call came in.

Caleb gave me a knowing smile. "Point proven. Answer it. Go on and save the world, Maisie. Just don't forget to eat." He dropped me a wink as I mouthed a thank you, before taking the call and closing the door.

FIFTEEN

Maisie

AT SOME POINT during a very long night, an idea hatched. I would wake up early and surprise Caleb at the start of his day with coffee and breakfast. Then, after a quick internet search and some hunting around, I discovered I could book space on all the tours he had going out tomorrow. Which I did, grinning like an idiot at his inefficient website. That man really needed to step into this decade!

Because *my* work ruined our first real day together, surprising him at *his* work so we could spend our entire second day together seemed a fitting way to make things up to him. Sure, we would be surrounded by tourists and he would be occupied doing whatever it was he did every day, but we'd still be together and then, as soon as the boat pulled up to the dock at precisely six pm (according to the dinosaur he called a website) the evening would be ours.

As I pulled the covers up around me sometime after two in the morning, I hoped my sudden arrival at the dock wouldn't seem too stalker-ish, then laughed off the thought. He was the one that asked (read: demanded) that I stay in the Keys in the first place. Aggression and directness seemed to be the name of the game between us. Which was good. I appreciated directness.

Obviously, I slept through my first alarm. And my second. So there wasn't a whole lot of time to get ready when I finally rolled out of bed. I pulled on a swimsuit and sundress, then took a peek in the mirror. My hair had gone wavy after being drenched in rainwater. Normally, I would straighten or curl it into submission, but there was something kind of nice about the relaxed waves, doing what they wanted to do. I didn't have time for makeup, so I washed my face and called it good enough.

I wouldn't dream of leaving my apartment like this in Los Angeles. Too much was riding on me being professional and presentable at any given juncture. But things moved at a slower pace here and as I slipped outside, the sun just barely peeking above the horizon and the wind from the ocean causing my hair to dance around my shoulders, I had to admit, it felt...nice.

Using the map on my phone, I located what looked like a decent coffee shop and grabbed us some go-juice and grub, then made my way to the marina as the sun started its trek into the sky. I kept the radio off, allowing my thoughts to keep me company as I continued to check off all the ways Los Angeles differed from the Keys.

More relaxed. Check.

Slower paced. Check.

Filled with memories, both good and bad. Check.

Had people who cared about me...

That last thought was a surprise. Surely I believed people cared about me in LA. I was Brighton's maid of honor. Several of my clients owed their entire career to me. But I thought through the list of people surrounding me back home and all I really ended up with was that solitary plant waiting for me on the shelf next to Caleb's picture. And that wasn't even a people.

Hmmm.

But who did I think cared about me here? Caleb, obviously. I expected the list to end there, but my brain went right ahead and ticked down the rest of his family, even though I had only seen them once, for a few hours, yesterday.

"And Eli wasn't even there," I reminded myself, only for my head to insist he would have been just as excited to see me as the rest of the Hutton crew.

The thoughts were equal parts comforting and unsettling. Was I lonely? Was I *actually* lonely, living the dream in the city of angels? It didn't seem like that could be right—I was literally surrounded by people out there—but the more I thought about it, the more I could see the truth.

I, Maisie Brown, reverser of fortunes, luck amplifier to the up and coming best and brightest, was lonely.

Well, okay then.

I turned on the radio for the rest of the trip and focused on how surprised Caleb would be when I finally arrived. My plan had been to beat him there, but I pulled up beside his convertible just as he killed the engine. He turned to me, a pair of aviators making him look utterly delectable.

"Hey, you," I called as I stood, holding out the coffee like a peace offering.

A wide grin broke across his face. "Well hey there, beautiful." He stood, closed the door, and met me in front of the vehicle. One arm snaked around my waist as he drew me close. "I didn't expect to see you today."

"Yeah, well, surprise! I didn't get enough of you yesterday. My fault! I know. Work, work, work. I'm a living breathing Rihanna song." I grinned, hoping he spent enough time in this decade to get the joke. "I thought I'd make up for it today. I am officially all yours."

Caleb frowned and stepped back, looking as dejected as a teenaged boy watching his crush dance with someone else. "I'll be on the water until six. I'm sorry, May-bell. I thought I said that yesterday."

"You did." I nodded enthusiastically. "And I'll be on the water with you. I have officially booked all your tours, even though your website is a more of an antique than your phone."

It was difficult to read his expression through his sunglasses, but I thought he looked pleased. "You expect me to be able to concentrate on work with you looking like that? For that matter, how in the world am I going to be able to flirt with all the ladies?"

"Is that your secret to success? Slap on a fake accent, flash those muscles and that smile, then rake in the moola?"

"You forgot my charming charisma."

I pulled back to slap him on the arm. "And your unwavering confidence."

"Obviously. Tools of the trade, Maisie. I feel like you should know this." Caleb took a long pull of his coffee and shook his head. "Well, come on then. You're here early enough, you can help me get the boat ready, if you're interested in learning how to handle the ropes."

I could handle his rope all day long. "I am at your disposal, Cap'n," I said with a little salute. "Tell me where you want me and I'm all yours."

He stopped in his tracks and turned to me, sliding off his aviators so I could see the devilish look glinting in his playful eyes. "Careful what you say, there. You never know how someone might take it."

"Look at you. So sure I said that on accident. Aren't you cute?" With that, I sauntered on ahead of him, reveling in his deep, appreciative laughter before I turned back. "Oh. I almost forgot," I said as I held out my phone with a flourish. "This will not be joining us today." I pulled open the door to my rental and slipped my phone inside the glove box before locking the doors and tossing the keys into my bag. "I am officially yours."

Caleb draped an arm around my shoulder and pulled me close. "But that's nothing new," he said. "You've always been mine."

He smiled, and I laughed, and somewhere, deep inside my heart, I recognized the truth of his words. For a moment, I worried about the impossibility of our situation before burying those fears in a box in the back of my mind.

Today was ours and nothing was going to get in the way of that.

SIXTEEN

Caleb

HAVING Maisie on the boat with me all day was better than I could have imagined. I used her as a model when I demonstrated how to use the gear. She sipped on drinks as I steered the boat through the water. Sometimes we talked, and sometimes we just sat together, enjoying each other's company. I frequently found her staring at me, looking both happy and sad. The moment she caught me watching her, the look would vanish and I'd be left wondering what was going on in her head.

She was even more beautiful today than she had all week. All the LA polish had worn off last night, leaving nothing but her pretty features on display. Her blond hair hung in soft waves down her back, free to move as she turned her head. Her warm, blue eyes stood out from her natural face. Somehow, the makeup she usually wore took away from her beauty and I wondered if she knew how little effort she needed to actually be stunning.

She watched as I fielded drunken questions and selfie requests, catching my gaze with wide eyes. "Cap'n Caleb has real star power," she said during a moment of quiet.

"I like to have fun. People appreciate that."

"Sure, like your stunning good looks have nothing to do with it."

I brushed off the compliment. "It's the accent and you know it."

At the end of the day, she helped me get the boat back into the marina, securing her to the dock while I shut everything down. All in all, having Maisie around was easy and made a wonderful day even better. It was like she turned up the volume on all the stuff I normally enjoyed. I said as much as we made our way back to the parking lot and she laughed.

"So this will sound weird, but back home...I kind of consider myself a luck amplifier." She blushed in a rare moment of embarrassment and looked down at her feet, as the wind blew her hair into her face. I tucked a strand behind her ear. She leaned into the touch and glanced up at me. "Maybe I'm just an amplifier," she offered with a delicate smile.

"Maybe," I replied. "Seems like it to me, anyway. Things are just better when you're around."

Again, the next logical question would be *so how long are you going to be around, anyway?* But I didn't want to ruin the moment, so I shoved the question away.

I was breaking all my rules to be with her. Nothing short-term. No one-night stands. No tourists.

But this was Maisie.

Did she really count as short-term? Did she really count as a tourist? She had a permanent spot in my heart. She had since we were kids and even thirteen years without contact hadn't changed that. Surely she wouldn't head back home and disappear from my life again. Right? Surely, she was more than a one-night stand...if things ever came to that.

My arousal sprang to life, reminding me how I very much wanted it to come to that. I wanted her body. I wanted her time and her attention. I wanted her back in my life.

We arrived at our vehicles and she paused next to hers, hands clasped in front of her, bright smile in place. "I really enjoyed watching you work, Cap'n."

"I really enjoyed watching you."

Her eyes bounced around my face, pleasure

lighting her up from the inside out and I knew in that moment that I didn't care about the rules. I didn't care about anything but her. "Hungry? I know a great place..." I began but Maisie was already nodding her head.

"Yep. Starving." She hooked her arm through my elbow. "Take me to dinner or lose me forever."

I frowned down at her, disappointed that she massacred one of my favorite lines from *Top Gun*. "I don't think that's how it goes."

"Well, sure. That's not what Meg Ryan says to Goose, but I'm not Meg Ryan, and you're a Moose, not a goose..." She grimaced, then let out a ridiculous laugh. "I'm sorry," she said through her giggles. "In my head, that sounded really clever. Out loud, it was just bad."

I laughed with her. "Oh Maisie. And here I actually thought this had a chance of working out."

"Really? You're going to let one bad joke ruin this for you?" she asked as I opened the passenger door on the Fairlane.

I pretended to think it through as I walked around the front and sat behind the wheel. "Maybe. Maybe not. I think we'll see how the rest of the evening goes before I make a final call."

"Who says you're the one making any calls?"

"Oh come on, May-bell. You know I've always

been in charge of our adventures." I brought the engine to life. "Now, sit back, enjoy the ride, and never, *ever* massacre *Top Gun* again."

I TOOK Maisie to one of my favorite restaurants—a casual place with an ocean view and great food. We laughed. We drank. We ate. We shared stories about work and life and the more she let her guard down, the more I knew I was utterly helpless in this situation. Even though I knew she was temporary, she already had a permanent place in my heart.

She was beautiful and intelligent and sure, she would be leaving soon, but at that point, I really didn't care. I'd deal with that heartache later because reconnecting with her was much better than spending the rest of my life wondering what could have been.

"You know," Maisie said, running a finger through the condensation on her glass. "I haven't felt this free in a long time. Honestly, I didn't know I *wasn't* feeling free until today." She glanced up, her gaze soft and vulnerable.

"How so?"

"It's difficult to explain. The thought is so new, I'm just now starting to understand it. But..." She frowned as she folded her arms on the table and leaned closer.

"When I set out to find my career, I thought I'd find kids like me. Kids who were struggling. Kids whose parents weren't able to care for them for some reason or another. Kids who felt lost and alone. And I wanted to put them on a path to success. I wanted to lift up the downtrodden—you know, leave the world a better place than I found it."

"And you're not doing that now?"

"I mean, yes. In a way. But sometimes, it feels like I lift them up only to watch them combust a year or two down the road. Fame isn't easy and most people don't realize they're not cut out for it." She closed her eyes and visibly tried to shake off the thoughts. "I don't know what's gotten into me lately. Maybe I'm feeling guilty because I'm letting people down by staying here. Sorry to be such a drag," she said, opening her eyes with a grimace.

"You're not a drag. You are officially the opposite of a drag. And you don't have to stay, you know. The last thing I want to do is create a problem for you." The words were hard to say because the greedy side of me never wanted her to leave, but if being here was adding stress to her already stressful life, then I would be an asshole if I didn't let her go.

"That's the thing." Maisie smiled. "I don't want to go home. I like the way it feels here, and I am more surprised to admit that than anyone. I never thought

I'd want to be this close to where I grew up ever again."

I nodded my understanding. "Because of how things were when we were kids."

"I thought I left it all behind me. I thought I shed it like an old skin. When Brighton wanted to come back here, I braced myself. My new life meeting my old life seemed like this giant tragedy waiting to happen."

I wondered what she would say now that she was here. Did it still feel like a tragedy, the two of us sitting at a table for hours, lost in conversation about who we were, who we became, and where we wanted to go? "Do they know?" I asked. "Does anyone in Los Angeles know how life used to be for you?"

Maisie threw her head back and laughed. "God no. Could you imagine what Brighton would think if she knew who I was?"

"Wouldn't she think you were extra amazing for getting to where you are? When you had to start a mile behind everyone else? Seems like a logical progression of thoughts to me."

"If Brighton knew where I came from, she would see that we never really existed on the same level and that would be that. Friendship over."

"Then she's not much of a friend, is she?"

Maisie dipped her chin toward her shoulder. "Maybe that's part of what has me feeling so off. No one out there really knows me. Not the real me, anyway. I thought that was the way I wanted it." She lifted her drink with a shrug then took a sip. "Or maybe it's just the difference in the way I feel about you versus the way I feel about everyone else."

She looked like she was swimming in thoughts so deep she was on the verge of drowning. Like cracks were creeping up her foundation, ready to rattle her to her core. So, while I thought there was still much more she needed to talk about on this subject, I had no intention of pushing forward. Not with her so fragile. Sometimes healing came easiest in parts and pieces instead of a heavy dose of change taken all at once.

I lifted my drink and drawled in my best voice, "Here's to being the best at what I do."

Maisie burst into laughter. "You're just as bad as everyone out there, you know. With that fake accent and charming smile."

"The smile I can't help. That's just me being me. But the accent? There's nothing LA about it."

Maisie almost looked relieved by my statement. "That only proves you're just as capable of fooling yourself as anyone," she said, pointing a finger my way, pleased to have me by the balls. "The accent is no different than any actress getting plastic surgery to further her career. You're playing a part, just like everybody else."

"True." I sat back in my chair, ready to hit her with a dose of truth. "But those nose jobs? They only serve to better the lives of the people getting them. My accent isn't for me."

"Sure. You go ahead and keep telling yourself that." Maisie laughed and took a long drink, holding my gaze over the rim of her glass.

"Think about it, May-bell. You saw how people smiled when I talked to them on the boat today. They come down here to get a break from their busy lives, looking to let off some steam, and it brightens their day to have Cap'n Caleb doing his thing. I only use my fake accent for the powers of good. I promise."

"Uh-huh..." Maisie's smile seemed so genuine, I was glad I steered the conversation away from deeper waters. We would have to navigate the turbulence sooner or later, but she hadn't looked even remotely prepared to dive into the deep end. The last thing I wanted to be was the guy who ruined her perfect life by making her see all the ways it let her down.

SEVENTEEN

Maisie

TIME FLOWED AWAY as Caleb and I enjoyed each other's company. When dinner was over, the glasses were empty, and the bill was paid, I was still nowhere near done drinking him in.

"What?" he asked, tilting his head quizzically.

"Just thinking."

"That much was obvious. Hence my question." He rolled his hands through the air as his blue eyes lit up with happiness. "What, exactly, are you thinking about?"

"You. Us." I shrugged because that one word held so many implications. *Us.* Could there even be an us once this fairytale of a vacation was over? Smiling, I said what was on my mind. "I'm not ready for this to end."

The statement was true on many levels. I wasn't ready for our dinner to end. I wasn't ready for my time in Key West to end. And I wasn't ready for whatever this was growing between Caleb and me to end.

"Me neither." Caleb's eyes brimmed with emotion and I could have sworn he was also speaking on many levels. "Feel like coming to my house?"

The answer was simple, just like everything else about being with him.

Yes, yes, yes, yes, yes.

His house was small but tidy, tucked away off the beaten path with a private beach and a hammock stretching between palms. The wraparound porch reminded me of a smaller version of The Hut. All that was missing were the ferns, the Adirondack chairs, and the memories.

Caleb held open the front door, reaching in to flick on the lights as I stepped inside. "It's nothing special," he said, moving easily into his home. "But it works for me."

I surveyed the space. Older furniture—clean but broken in. Bare walls, save a few family pictures. One of a younger Caleb caught my attention, his body still in the process of filling out, standing in front of his boat with a grin stretching across his face.

"That was the day I bought her," he said, sneaking up behind me and wrapping an arm around my waist, drawing me close so my back was pressed to his front. "I was so proud."

"I can see it." I turned in his arms, so we were face to face. "And you had every right to be proud of yourself."

Realization hit me as I stared into his eyes, darkening with desire. I was in his house. In his arms. And there was no way we would have a drink or two and call it a night. When he invited me here, it was for one reason. And when I accepted, it was because I knew that reason. And suddenly, I found myself feeling afraid.

"Everything about you breaks my rules," I said, dropping my gaze because I couldn't withstand the look on his face much longer. He was lust personified, burning with need, sending fire winging through my veins. "I'm a no strings attached kind of girl."

"And I have strings?" Caleb's low voice held an undercurrent of implications.

"Of course you have strings." I met his eyes again. "You're...you."

He licked his lips. "You don't exactly fit into my rulebook, either. I'm not into tourists. Or one-night stands. I'm not a short-term kind of guy."

"So what does it mean? Are we making a mistake?"

Caleb pulled me even closer, angling his mouth over mine. "No," he said as he leaned in. "Yes." His kissed the corner of my lips, then cupped my cheeks, pulling away to meet my gaze. "Honestly, I don't really care anymore."

In that moment, I agreed with him. This was both a terrible idea and a wonderful thing and I didn't have it in me to unravel it all. I turned my head and kissed him full on, losing myself to the heat of his touch. Caleb backed me up, capturing me between his body and the wall, running his hands up my waist, kneading my breast as my nipples pebbled at his touch.

"Tell me, May-bell," he breathed as his erection pressed into my belly. "Does this feel like a mistake?"

I shook my head. "Not even a little bit."

He tugged my shirt over my head and buried his face between my breasts, kissing and sucking until I was sure he had marked me. I moaned my appreciation, my body responding to his with an urgency that felt like coming up for air. With the love I felt for him when we were children coloring every decision I ever made, Caleb's mark was already on my soul. It felt right to have him physically marking me, too.

I fumbled with his shirt, desperate to feel his skin on mine, to have access to all of him. Finally, I managed to get it off and tossed it on the floor while he unburdened me of the rest of my clothes, then kneeled in front of me, hooking one leg over his shoulder. He worked magic with his tongue, while he slipped a finger inside, working my body into a frenzy.

Looking down at him, on his knees before me, his face buried between my thighs...seeing him there was a pleasure I couldn't name. My muscles quivered and danced and I gripped his blond hair, both trying to bring him closer and keep him from pushing me over an edge that seemed impossibly high. Slowly, decadently, he energized my buzzing nerves until need for him overwhelmed me.

"Caleb..." I breathed his name as my eyes rolled shut. "Please..."

My hips began to buck as I imagined him inside me, thrusting and groaning, his pleasure heightening mine and mine heightening his in an ever-spiraling dance of gratification. What he was doing felt amazing, but I wanted *him*.

He stood, wiping his mouth with the back of his hand. "Please what?"

"Take me to your bedroom or lose me forever." I smirked and his eyes went wide.

"What did I tell you about massacring lines from *Top Gun?*" With that, he swooped me up and tossed me over his shoulder, lightly smacking my ass while I squealed with laughter. His hand stroked over the swell of my bottom, then slipped between my legs.

When we reached his bedroom, he lowered me onto the mattress.

With humor twinkling in his sexy eyes, he stepped out of his shorts then spun them in a circle over his head while swinging his hips. The muscles in his abdomen flexed with the movement and the long line of his dick stood out proudly through his boxer briefs. I laughed at his stripper impersonation as he let his shorts fly, then gasped as he stepped out of the briefs. He was magnificent, his cock long and proud and perfectly shaped.

Caleb climbed onto the bed, spreading my thighs with his knees while I reached between us to wrap my hand around his hot, velvety length. Moisture dripped from his tip and I swirled my thumb around it, dipping low to stroke the soft indentation under the head.

He made a low sound of approval in the back of his throat. "Fuck, that feels good." He dropped his head back and closed his eyes and my lower belly throbbed with need.

I wanted him inside me. I wanted him buried deep. I wanted him shaping me. Stretching me. Erasing any and all space between us, until we were working toward one goal, as one person, pleasing each other above all things. He reached into his bedside drawer and pulled out a condom, tearing the foil and slipping it into place. I watched hungrily as he readied himself for me, then gripped the back of my head and lowered me to the bed, kissing me deeply as he lined himself up and slid inside.

Fireworks of pleasure lit up the backs of my eyelids. My body sang the Hallelujah chorus and somewhere, a voice whispered *finally* as I murmured, "Oh, fuck." And then Caleb started moving, his hands and his lips working in concert with his magnificent dick.

We were a symphony. A work of art. Perfectly choreographed harmony wrapped up in dirty words and filthy mouths. He ravished me and I rode him, and the frenzy of our need ended in one desperate shout on his part and a long moan of completion from me as I dropped back on the bed.

Caleb lowered himself beside me, pushing my hair out of my eyes. I turned to him, a wide perma-grin etched into my face. "We just ruined sex for the rest of the world, you know that?"

He laughed lightly and propped his head up with his hand. "How so?"

"No one can ever match what we just did. We set the sex-bar so high, no couple will ever live up to it. And they all know it. Even if they don't know they know...they know. There's no way everyone in the whole wide world didn't feel what just happened. It was that good. That perfect. That..." I ran out of words, realizing it was impossible to explain the connection between us. It defied explanation. It just *was*.

He beamed, looking satisfied and happy and so damn handsome he gave every leading man through all the ages a run for his money, and something inside me shifted. The feeling was small, but monumental. It was lovely and terrifying, and completely inevitable.

We were connected, he and I. Strings firmly attached. A tangle of implications and expectations and as I curled into him, pressing my cheek against his firm chest as he ran a hand through my hair, tears formed in my eyes, though I couldn't say for sure why.

EIGHTEEN

Maisie

THE NEXT MORNING, the light purr of Caleb's snores pulled me from sleep. I rolled over and studied his face, appreciating the reddish tint to the stubble growing on his cheeks and chin, the gentle upturn of his nose, his full lips. What we did last night was...

What was it?

Wonderful. Inevitable. Magical. Pornographic. Life-altering.

Little bells went off inside my head on that last one. *Ding, ding, ding! Fifty points to Miss Brown! Life-altering is the correct answer!*

Nothing could be the same after last night. We had buried friendship under passion and flipped short-term sex-cations the bird. After what we did, there was a permanence about us that defied our reality.

Caleb shifted, throwing an arm over his head and sighing in his sleep. I smiled as I slid out of bed, stopping to pull on my undies and his shirt before I padded out of the room in search of coffee.

My purse lurked on the floor near the door, heavy with the threat of a bajilllionty angry texts, emails, and voicemails from Los Angeles. I stopped to fish out my phone, swiping away the messages without looking at them on my way to the kitchen. If I had any lingering doubts that Caleb and I were perfect together, his Keurig station knocked them straight out of my head. Neatly organized and packed with variety, it was a delightful blend of chaos and harmony. I picked out a pod and popped it into the machine, then tapped out a message to Brighton as I waited for my cup to fill.

It happened.

She wouldn't need more information than that to know what I was talking about, and her reply only confirmed my confidence in her ability to read between the lines.

No freaking way!

She followed that one up with a string of emojis. An eggplant. A peach. A face with heart eyes. They devolved from there and I rolled my eyes at her enthusiasm.

I can't believe you had sex with your picture frame boy. Wait. Yes. Yes. I can. How was it?

I let that question roll around in my head for a bit while I took my first few sips of coffee. I didn't think she wanted a play by play, and I wasn't one to share details like that anyway. Finally, I went with the truth.

Life-altering.

Brighton replied with another string of emojis, which meant she was distracted. Considering it was ten in the morning on a weekday—which made it just barely seven for her—she had to be gearing up to be knee deep in crisis. I picked up my phone to tell her I'd talk to her later, when a new message buzzed in.

It's a shitshow here, thank you very much. I'm running in place, trying to put out fires for you. So, you know, don't be shocked if you come back and find half of your clients interested in breaking your contract to sign with me.

She followed that up with a winky face, supposedly to show she was being funny, but somehow, the text felt more like a threat than a joke. I picked through the selection of coffee, wondering which one Caleb liked most, and waited for the surge of emotion to hit me in response to Brighton's barb. Nothing happened, which I chalked up to the magical sexcapades from the night before. Smiling, I grabbed a pod I thought Caleb would appreciate and dropped it into the Keurig before typing out one last text to Brighton.

Thanks for running defense. If you get a chance...would you water my plant for me?

I didn't expect a response, but got one anyway.

Sure thing, chica. Happy sexy times!

Part of me had expected her to ask how I ended up running into Caleb at that bar. I know *my* curiosity would be piqued, if the situation were reversed. It was too big a coincidence that of all the bars in all the world, he and I ended up in the same one. The only logical conclusion was that I had grown up around here and had never mentioned it the entire time Brighton planned her wedding. Which, if it were me, would set off a whole slew of red flags. Maybe she assumed it was a massive coincidence, or maybe she just didn't care that much. Either way, I was tired of wasting energy on worrying about her.

I considered opening up my messages and wading into the shitshow to help put out the fires, but damn it. I didn't want work to color my time with Caleb. Without another thought, I powered down my phone and set it aside, leaning my elbows on the counter to blow into my coffee.

"Sweet baby Jesus, you are a sight to behold."

Caleb's voice came from behind me and I glanced over my shoulder to find him leaning against the wall, sporting a pair of low-slung sweatpants and nothing else. A light spattering of golden hair sprinkled his chest and trailed down his abdomen, disappearing into his waistline.

"Wearing my shirt," he continued. "With it showing so much of those legs..."

I straightened and turned as he made his way to me, lifting me onto the counter and stepping into the space between my thighs. He buried his face in my chest and I smoothed his sleep-crazed hair. His body was still warm from being in bed and contentment melted the tension in my shoulders.

"I made you a cup of coffee," I murmured.

Caleb made a sound that could have been a hum of approval, or perhaps was a moan of displeasure at being awake, then lifted a grabby hand. I chuckled and retrieved his mug and settled it into his palm.

"Bless you, child," he said, then sat up enough to take a long swig.

"Not one for mornings?" I asked.

"Not even a little." He took another long drink. "You?"

I shrugged. The truth was, I didn't sleep much at all, staying up too late, waking up frequently during the night, and then finally deciding to stay awake sometime before my alarm went off each morning. "This is the latest I've slept in a long time. You're the best stress relief I've found yet."

His eyes met mine, a slow smile pulling at his lips. "I'm just that good," he said.

"And modest," I replied.

"Oh, yes. Modesty is my strongest trait." He took another long pull of his coffee and set his mug next to mine. "Now, for the most important question of the morning. Do you fish?"

"The closest I ever got was when we were kids and I'd sit and watch you fish off the dock at The Hut."

"Interested?" he asked, looking hopefully skeptical.

"Honestly, no." I laughed. "Like, imagine you're a fish, just swimming about, thinking you're about to have a delightful snack when suddenly a hook jams through your lips and you're jolted into a world where you can't breathe and giant monsters manhandle you."

Caleb stared at me with wide eyes. "That's...descriptive."

"But if you want to fish today, don't let me hold you back. I'd be happy to sit and watch you."

"And judge me as a giant monster manhandling fish."

I winked. "Yeah. But, that never stopped you before..."

I watched as he understood what I was saying.

Incredulity painted surprise on his face and next thing I knew, he was chasing me into the living room. "I'll show you a giant monster," he said as I squealed in protest.

"I'm pretty sure you already showed me last night." I darted around the couch, hoping to make a break for the back door, but Caleb out-maneuvered me and pulled me in for a kiss.

"I'll show you again tonight, too. And tomorrow. And the next day." He trailed off, a question dancing through his eyes. I knew what it was. *How long are you staying?*

But I didn't know the answer and he didn't ask, so I kissed him again, distracting him by reaching down to stroke his giant monster, then made a break for the door.

NINETEEN

Caleb

WHEN WE WERE KIDS, Maisie used to spend a lot of time at my house. Both our dads were drunks, but mine tended to hole up in his office and there were plenty of places to be at The Hut that kept us out of his line of fire. Maisie's house was small and she had nowhere to go to get a break from Mr. Brown, except to me. Some days she needed distraction from her anxious energy, so, I would create an adventure for us, one that had us running along the beaches, exploring worlds only in our imaginations.

Other times, she needed quiet. Those were the days I would invite her to sit on the dock with me while I fished. She would dangle her feet in the water and stare at the horizon while I enjoyed her quiet company. After Maisie left for Kentucky and I grew, I wondered if I had imagined the different ways she needed me. If those ideas were nothing more than a little boy thinking he knew more than he did, but today, looking at her as she led me in a chase around my house and right out the back door to stare at the ocean, I knew I'd been right on the money.

Somehow, back then, I had been able to understand what she needed, maybe better than she ever did. And it was no different now.

I stepped up behind her and wrapped my arms around her waist, drawing her against my body and peering at the water over her shoulder. "I'm surprised how much I missed it," she said quietly.

I kissed her cheek. "I'm not." We stayed like that for some time, me wrapped around her as if I could physically protect Maisie from whatever was bothering her. Her leaning into me, borrowing my strength as we swayed slightly, watching the waves wash up on the beach. She yawned, then excused herself, sounding almost embarrassed about such a natural human reaction.

"You want to take a nap?" I asked, then had a natural human reaction of my own at the thought of having her in my bed again.

Maisie giggled, wriggling her hips so her ass rubbed

against my poor, straining dick. "Is that what we're calling it now? Napping?" She turned a little and made air quotes around her last word.

"Hell, woman. You are insatiable." Though, I was too, when it came to her. With anyone else, I'd have had my fill, my body urging me to take a break and get some rest. With Maisie, it was like we knew the clock was ticking down on our time together, and we were bound and determined to make as much of what we had as we could.

"I didn't get to where I am by taking it easy." She stepped out of my arms and turned to face me. A hungry gleam set into her eyes. "And there's no way I could sleep, knowing this thing was waiting for me." She ran a hand along my erection.

"Then we'll sleep after." I took her hand and led her back through my house and into my bedroom where we wore each other out, before Maisie curled into me and fell fast asleep.

I DIDN'T STAY ASLEEP LONG, and quietly slipped from my bed, pausing to stare down at Maisie's sweet face as she got some much needed rest, the space between her brows relaxed and easy as her hair fanned out on my pillow. I decided to take today easy, to give her some time to regain her energy and recoup her reserves. She slept for a couple hours and finally emerged from my bedroom looking sexy as hell, still wearing only my shirt.

We watched some Netflix as we ate leftovers for a late lunch, my shock at her utter lack of knowledge around pop culture growing with each show she swore she had never seen.

"For someone who works in show business, you have some serious holes in your education." I stared at her, shaking my head. "How do you even live on this planet?"

"I'm too busy actually working to sit down and watch TV," she replied, as if that proved some kind of point.

"Yeah? And how is that working out for you?" I meant it as a joke around the fact that she hadn't seen some of this decade's most popular shows, but her gaze darted to her cellphone—powered down and hunkered on my counter like a snake waiting to strike.

"It's working out very well," she said with a proud smile. "I live a very fulfilling life."

After that, she got quiet again, so I turned on a comedy, wrapped an arm around her shoulder, and drew her in close. We stayed like that for several hours, laughing until we cried, until she finally pushed into a sitting position, stretching her arms toward the ceiling.

"What time is it?" she asked, stifling yet another yawn. "Are you hungry? I think I'm hungry."

"I could eat," I said, as my stomach rumbled its approval of the idea.

"Yeah, but something tells me that's just your natural state."

I bobbed my head. "This is true. What sounds good? We could order in, if you want."

Maisie wrinkled her nose and I found myself doubting everything I thought I knew. Had I been wrong about her needing to hibernate a little to regain her energy? Had we spent one of our precious days lounging on the couch in my boring house because I thought I was saving her, and she was actually bored to tears?

"Can you cook?" she asked.

"No," I replied with a laugh. "Can you?"

"Hell no. But..." She gave me a cautious look. "Today has been so nice and relaxing. I almost always eat carry out and it sounded pretty wonderful to cook a meal and eat it here. You know. Like a normal person."

I wasn't sure how many normal people ate home-cooked meals in this day and age, but I didn't say that to her. "Let's give it a try. We're two reasonably intelligent adults. How hard could it be to follow a recipe?"

Turned out, it could be pretty hard. After a quick trip to the store to pick up supplies, we let ourselves get

cocky as we chopped vegetables and readied the ingre-
dients for a salad to go with our lasagna. Browning the
meat wasn't all that difficult, either. Neither was
boiling the water for the noodles. But the assembly of
said lasagna went horribly wrong and by the time we
sat down to eat the monstrosity we created, we were
laughing so hard our sides cramped.

"It's the ugliest thing I've ever seen," she said,
wiping tears from the corners of her eyes.

"Yeah. Poor old Bertha won't be winning any
beauty contests."

Maisie looked at me incredulously, mouthing the
name, before she burst out in another fit of laughter.
When we regained control, we toasted to Bertha and
dug in. While she wasn't much to look at, the lasagna
tasted delicious, and we moaned our appreciation at
our handiwork until our bellies were so full we thought
they would burst.

Maisie sat back in her chair and let out a long sigh.
"You always did know how to make me feel better," she
said. "Today was everything I needed and I didn't even
know I needed it."

I lifted my wineglass. "To us."

Maisie frowned. Then smiled. Then nodded as she
lifted her glass as well. "To us."

TWENTY

Maisie

TO US.

The words sounded sweet and tasted bitter.

As wonderful as today had been...

As much as I needed the time to lounge around doing nothing...

As perfect as Caleb was...

...he was medical marijuana and I didn't partake.

This life, sleeping until ten, hanging out in comfy clothes, watching TV on the couch, it wasn't mine. I didn't make monstrous lasagnas because I didn't have time. (Not to mention in LA, that kind of reckless indulgence in carbs was highly frowned upon.) My clients needed me to be in their corners, fighting for their dreams, and that meant I didn't get to spend days with my phone turned off.

With *me* turned off.

But I'd had such a lovely time and couldn't imagine saying what was on my mind, so I smiled, lifted my glass, and toasted to us.

To beautiful, poetic, short-lived us.

"Do you remember Fort Maileb?" I asked as I set my glass down on the table.

Caleb smirked. "I think you mean Fort Casie."

His answer brought another smile to my lips. "Oh no," I said, wagging my finger. "I very much mean Fort Maileb. It was my idea to join our names together, so obviously, my name got to go first."

"Sure, it was your idea. But I was the one who found all the scrap wood *and*"—he held up a finger—"I'm the one who knew how to use a hammer and nails, so clearly, that meant my name earned the place up front."

"You call what you did knowing how to use a hammer and nails?" I dropped him a wink, then leaned back and took another drink, remembering the grove next to Caleb's house where he and I had built ourselves a sanctuary from the rest of the world. A place where no one could call our dreams dumb, or make fun of us for my clothes or his body. A place where we could say what we were thinking without fear of judgement or criticism. "You think it's still there?"

Caleb shook his head. "Dad bought that land a year or two after you left to expand the hotel. Nothing but bungalows there now."

I rolled my eyes. "I guess I should have known that. I was there just the other day and saw zero groves."

"Eh." Caleb shrugged. "There's been a lot going on."

I lifted my glass. "To understatements."

He agreed with a chuckle, then polished off his wine and stood to start clearing the table. We worked side by side again, moving around each other as if we'd done it for years, already comfortable sharing a space.

"How come you don't work with your family at The Hut?" I leaned on the counter to watch his reaction. "It seems like you would be a great asset there. And with that cove as a tourist spot? Could you imagine? That is pure gold, right there."

Caleb finished loading the dishwasher and turned to me. "Wyatt offered once. Before I started my own business. But, I had washed my hands of Dad and wanted nothing to do with him, so I said no thank you and forged ahead on my own."

That sounded very much like an adult version of

the kid I remembered. I always respected his ability to cut through it all and see his place in the world, something I taught myself to emulate shortly after my family moved to Kentucky. "You always had a clear vision of who you are and what you want."

Caleb snorted. "I think most people would describe me as stubborn and hard-headed."

"Well, sure. Those things go hand in hand with knowing who you are and what you want. Don't you know *anything* about how the world works?"

It was so easy being with him. We shared the same sense of humor. Had the kind of chemistry that scorched the earth around us. Felt immense appreciation for the simple things that so many took for granted...

It was just everything else about us that was different.

He drew me in close and pressed a kiss to my lips. "I know I like having you within arm's reach."

I liked it, too. Very much. Maybe even too much. I returned the kiss and then put some distance between us. "What about now that your dad's gone? Have you given any more thought about joining forces with the rest of your family and working at The Hut? Or has that ship sailed?"

Caleb gave me a funny look and very deliberately

stepped back into my space again. "If I didn't know any better, I'd say you're trying to distract me."

"And just why do you think I'd do that?"

"Because you're scared."

His words hit a little too close to the truth and I wasn't ready to get that kind of honest. Not yet. Maybe not ever. These moments with Caleb were just as precious as the ones in our past, but they weren't reality, and if we weren't careful, we were going to get hurt. Sometimes it felt like we were trying to cram in another childhood's worth of memories before I went home, while refusing to acknowledge the fact that I *was* going home. Even if we didn't want to, it was happening. Soon.

Instead of saying any of that, I laughed as if he had just made a Bertha level joke. "I mean, he's huge," I said as I palmed his dick, "but I don't think you've given me any reason to be scared."

He studied me for a long moment and I felt like he could see right through me. Like he could tell I was avoiding the scary stuff and hiding behind sex. Like he was going to call me on it and things were going to get very real, very fast. Expectation rose inside me. The conversation wouldn't be easy, but it was necessary. And maybe, just maybe, we could figure out a way to keep what we were building.

But then he pressed his hips into my hand, smiling

down at me. "Oh, I'll give you a reason to be scared all right," he said before scooping me up, throwing me over his shoulder, and carrying me back to his bedroom.

There was an insistence to our movements that night, a desperation that hadn't been there before. A frantic need that drove us forward, denying our awareness of the rest of the world. I dropped to my knees in front of him, taking his thick length in my hand, swirling my tongue around his tip. His hips pressed forward and I opened my mouth for him, moaning as he quivered in pleasure *I* was giving him. His hands fisted in my hair, holding me in place, his crown pressing against the back of my throat. I swallowed and the sound he made sent molten desire through my body.

To know I could make him feel that way, down on my knees and vulnerable to him, had me feeling powerful. I drew my tongue along the underbelly of his shaft, running my fingernails up his legs. He made another sound that had me throbbing with need, then helped me to my feet and out of my clothes.

"I'm sorry," he said. "That felt amazing, but I want all of you."

When he plunged into me, I dropped my head back onto the pillow and closed my eyes, but Caleb slid a hand around the nape of my neck and lifted my gaze to his. "Stay with me," he said. "Don't look away."

I met his gaze as his hips rolled into mine again and again. We finished together, our bodies unlocking as one and I fell asleep tucked into his arms, warm and content and safe next to him.

TWENTY-ONE

Maisie

THE NEXT DAY, Caleb had to work, so I went back to my room at The Hut. After all, the family had gone to the trouble of getting the place ready for me, the least I could do was spend a little time there. After a long soak in the tub of awesomeness, I curled up in a chair on the private patio and turned on my phone, bracing myself for the barrage of incoming missed calls and emails.

Whatever I expected, reality was worse. I flipped through the list without really reading them as anxiety flooded my system. How could one redheaded rock star cause so much chaos because I managed to get him a part in a movie? In what universe was this a bad thing?

There were people with hungry bellies, children living in warzones, families struggling to survive on the very same planet where Collin West was pissed off because he didn't have enough time onscreen.

It all seemed so inconsequential. So utterly ridiculous. But, by ignoring it all in favor of spending time with Caleb, I was putting my job at risk. And if I lost my job, I would lose everything.

I thumbed through the messages from Brighton, looking for anything that might resemble a message from a friend, but all I found were questions about work. There wasn't one single email, text, or call waiting for me on that phone that had anything to do with me as a person.

Maisie Brown wasn't a human being. She was a commodity.

I opened Facebook and scrolled through the list of waiting friend requests, all from faces I didn't recognize. My feed was filled with people who probably didn't even know my name and the same thing was waiting for me over on Instagram. I didn't even bother opening the app before I locked my phone and put it down.

Those messages could wait. Whatever was happening in Los Angeles wasn't life-threatening. They could go another day or two before I hopped back into solving other people's first world problems.

I was meeting Caleb back at his house that evening, so I spent the day shaving my legs, walking on the beach, and lounging in the sun. Cat—the hotel's masseuse—had a cancellation and offered me the time slot, which I happily took and sighed as her deft hands worked at untangling the knots of stress I carried in my shoulders.

"You seem so happy," she said. "I'm actually surprised to find you're hiding enough anxiety to do this." She pressed on a particularly painful spot on my back, then slowly started working out the knot.

"I'm just as surprised as you are, honestly," I replied, moaning a little as she kneaded the troublesome muscle. "I *am* happy."

Cat focused her attention on my back and I urged myself to relax under her skilled fingers. When she started speaking again, I almost missed it, her voice was so quiet. "Sometimes we're so busy trying to create a wonderful life, we don't realize how much of it is smoke and mirrors, lies we tell ourselves to get through the day without crying. At least that's what happened to me, before I met Lucas."

I let those words roll around in my head for a bit, trying to untangle how much of it applied to my life. Before I came to the Keys, I would have sworn I was happy. That I had it all. That my life was perfect in its fairytale-style, living-the-dream completeness. And now, in the span of just a few days, it felt like I'd been lying to myself the whole time. That the life I built was teetering on a weak foundation and that I was the same lost little girl I thought I had outgrown, the only difference was that now I wore designer shoes.

"Sheesh," Cat said as she worked into my back. "Just when I thought I was making progress, you go and get all tense again."

I did my best to relax. To focus on my breathing. To imagine all the good that I had. My mind went immediately to Caleb. Not my fancy office or my well-decorated apartment. Not to the connections I had cultivated with influential people in the business, but to the charming man with his old-fashioned phone and low-tech website. To Matthew McConaughey's love child with his ridiculous fake accent and cool-as-a-cucumber approach to life. I found myself smiling and Cat let out a sigh of relief.

"There we go," she said. "Now we're getting somewhere. Just keep breathing and doing what you're doing. Whatever it is, you're on the right track."

———

LATER THAT EVENING, I pulled up in front of Caleb's house and found him waiting for me on the steps. He stood as I killed the engine and climbed out of the car.

"There's the face I've been waiting all day to see," he said, opening his arms as I closed the distance between us. "How was your day?"

"Confusing," I said, before I could talk myself out of being honest.

"I had a feeling you were going to say that." Caleb pressed a kiss into my forehead and then tilted my chin up to meet his gaze. "I made you something."

"Made me something?"

A hint of embarrassment crossed his face as he smiled. "Yeah. Maybe it's silly. But it seemed...right." With that strange statement, Caleb took me by the hand and led me into his house.

There, taking up most of the living room, was a blanket fort. A giant, ridiculous, wonderful blanket fort with pillows spread out inside, a bottle of wine, and a picnic basket open and revealing dinner.

"You didn't..." I said, turning to him with a wide grin.

"Oh, I definitely did." He made a broad gesture with his arm. "Welcome to Fort Casie the Second."

"You know what? I'm so tickled that you went to all this trouble, that I'm not even going to fight you on the name." I dropped to my hands and knees and crawled inside, my purse slipping off my shoulder and dragging on the floor as I surveyed the space. "You thought of everything, didn't you?"

Caleb joined me, his large body brushing the blankets and sending a shudder of protest through the fort. "Mostly, I just thought of you."

"You are so amazing. Do you know that?" I leaned over to kiss him, breathing him in, desperate to have as much of him as I could before...before...

Caleb kissed me back with an urgency that matched mine, drawing me close and holding me tight, as if he never intended to let me go. "There's so much to talk about," he said when he finally released me. "And we've both been dancing around the hard topics. I thought this would make it easier to stop avoiding what we should have said days ago."

"God, you're perfect. It's no wonder I love you." The words slipped out so easily, so naturally, I barely had time to think about what I was saying.

He smiled sadly, questions dancing in his eyes. "That's the second time you said that, you know. That you love me."

"Yeah?" I drew my eyebrows together and tilted my head.

"Do you?" Caleb shifted, adjusting his long legs. "Do you love me?"

"Caleb...I've always loved you. How can you even ask me that?"

"Because the way a person loves their childhood friend is different than the way a man loves a woman."

"You're not wasting any time getting to those hard questions."

"We've already wasted enough time, don't you think?" Caleb reached for the bottle of wine and poured us each a glass. "Let's move on to an easier question, then," he said as he handed one to me. "Are you happy?"

I took a long drink as his first question bounced around in my brain. Did I love him? My heart answered the question without difficulty, the same way I had answered every question that came to Caleb.

Yes.

But was that residual love from when we were kids? Because of how he treated me? How he taught me to treat others? Or did I genuinely love him? The way a woman loves a man?

He was right, it was best to move on to easier questions. I gestured around Fort Casie the Second. "I'm a grown woman, sitting in a blanket fort with my best friend. How can I not be happy?"

"Take another drink, Masie."

I gave him a questioning look but Caleb refused to say anything more, simply gesturing at the full glass in my hand, so I did as he requested.

"Let's try this again without any of the bullshit.

Are you happy? Not just right now. But last year. Tomorrow. In this great and glorious life you have built, are you happy?"

This was getting serious. Quickly. I took yet another massive gulp of wine and let out a long sigh as I held out my glass for a refill. "I thought I was. I thought I had everything—the great mysteries of life and personal satisfaction—I thought I had it all figured out."

And just like that, the floodgates opened. I told him about Collin West and his ridiculous temper tantrum. I told him about my friendship with Brighton, how she knew Caleb was a childhood friend, but never even bothered to question how we came to end up as adults in the same bar. "Keep your friends close and your enemies closer," I said with a smirk. "I'm afraid that sums up my relationship with Brighton. I'm starting to think the only reason she's nice to me at all is because I'm her fiercest competition at Shift."

I told him about endless hours of work that I thought meant I was winning at life, and then I told him about lists and lists of so-called friends on my social media accounts. "I'm surrounded by people and feel completely and utterly alone. And within days of reuniting with you, it feels like everything I have is worth less, because you...you are worth so much more. You've made my life so full in such a short time, and it's made me realize how empty I really am." I finished that diatribe with another swig of wine.

Caleb echoed the motion, throwing back the drink like a shot, then refilling his glass.

"What about you?" I asked, desperate for a chance to breathe. "Are you happy?"

"I was perfectly content in my simple life. But now that I know what it's like to have you with me, I'm not sure how things will be when you leave. You're..." He shrugged. "It's always been you, Maisie. From the first time we met to the last time I saw you and all the years separating then from now, every woman has been held up to your standard and every woman has been found lacking. Why do you think I stay away from short-term? Because I'm looking for the meaning I had when you were in my life."

I shook my head, the rational side of me outright rejecting the thought that he could have spent his whole life loving me. We were just kids! How could I have had such a lasting impact on him?

And yet I'd spent my entire life loving him. *He* was my inspiration every time life got hard and I didn't know which way to go. His picture was the only personal item in my office. In fact, when you included the décor in my apartment, his picture was the only personal item in my life.

Caleb continued. "I didn't know I was doing it at

the time, obviously. Holding every woman I encountered up to your standard. It's only now, that you're here, that it's all made sense."

"So what happens when I leave?" My eyes met his and found all the fear and uncertainty I was feeling mirrored back at me.

"That's the question, isn't it?" he asked with a weak smile.

I took another drink, eyeing the dinner sitting untouched in the picnic basket. "You asked me if I love you. The answer is the same one I've been giving you since I've been here. You asked me to stay and I said yes. You asked me to dinner and I said yes. You asked me to come home with you and I said yes."

"And now I'm asking if you love me."

"And I'm saying yes." There hadn't been enough time to fall in love, and yet, we'd had our entire childhood. Adult Caleb fell so easily into his old place in my heart. He was still everything I needed. The ways he had grown and matured had done so hand in hand with the ways I had grown and matured and somehow, inexplicably, he was still my person. The one human being in existence to see all of me, to understand me, and to love me anyway.

Or at least I hoped he loved me anyway. It sounded like he loved me, but this wasn't a good time to make an assumption.

"Caleb...?"

"Yes, Maisie." He took my hand in his, already answering the question I hadn't yet asked. "Yes, I love you."

A trembling breath shuddered past my lips. The only way our love could work is by one of us giving up our life to move across the country for the other. After years of hard work, I had the financial security I prayed for—literally, every night—when I was a little girl. I no longer had to suffer through wanting something I needed. If something caught my eye, I bought it.

And yet...

I needed Caleb. And no amount of money could bring him into my life without tearing one of us out by the roots. If I chose to keep the life I had built with Shift, I would lose Caleb.

Everything I ever wanted at odds with everything I ever needed.

Fortune reversing over and over again.

A coin flipping through the air, our fate, our love caught in the balance.

"So, now what?" I asked.

"I guess it's time for the most important question of all." Hope tugged at the corners of his mouth, crinkling in the corners of his eyes. "How long are you staying, Maisie? How long do I have you?"

The question lingered between us. I was supposed

to leave days ago. We were already living on borrowed time. The answer was both *soon* and *forever*, both words caught in my throat because neither one made any sense.

My phone buzzed. "Shit," I said, reaching into my purse for the thing. "I forgot to set it on silent." Lombardi's name flashed across the screen, but I dismissed the call and silenced the phone. Before I had time to get my thoughts back in order, the screen lit up with another call, which I declined again.

Caleb gave me a sad smile. "Things are getting pretty bad for you, aren't they? Because I'm being so greedy."

A text came in. "I'm the one who took vacation time out of the blue. This isn't your fault." Another text. And another. I pressed a finger to the power button, eager to turn the stupid thing off though I knew that if Lombardi was calling, things were bad and ignoring him would only make things worse.

"Don't turn it off." Caleb shook his head. "I'll still be here when you're done solving whatever problem is on the other end of that line."

And so, when the phone lit up with one more call, I took a deep breath and answered.

TWENTY-TWO

Caleb

I POURED a glass of wine while Maisie got an earful from her boss. I drank said glass of wine, my eyes locked on hers, as I tried to ignore the stream of curse words that asshole flung her way. Maisie sat beside me in the blanket fort, shell-shocked, until finally she mouthed an apology, then turned her attention to the other man.

Her life was falling to pieces...all because I couldn't let her go. How selfish would I have to be, to expect her to keep ignoring her job, just because we happened to cross paths at a bar one night while she was on vacation? I hadn't canceled a single tour while Maisie was here, while she had been turning off her phone every time we got together. That wasn't balanced. Nor was it fair.

The problem was, and this was a big one...I couldn't help but be selfish. I wanted more of her. All of her. From the moment I built the blanket fort, my plan had been to ask her to stay. It was wrong to expect her to choose between her future and her past, but this was my last chance to keep her from walking out of my life forever. Again. I expected her to say no. What did she have here, other than me? I would respect that answer, because at my core, I understood, but I couldn't stop hoping that maybe, just maybe, she would say yes.

"Mr. Lombardi. You have no right to talk to me like that." Maisie opened her mouth to continue speaking and was interrupted by another stream of angry conversation.

"I had every right to take the time off. Everyone at Shift accrues personal days at the same rate, then wears that number like a badge of honor. I have ninety-six. Ninety-six personal days! Respectfully, I ask you to do the math on that. It's been a while since I've taken any time for myself." Maisie frowned, then climbed out of the fort, pinching the phone between her ear and her shoulder and putting her ass in my face on the way. Under any other circumstance, it would have been adorable. But under these particular circumstances, not so much.

It seemed Maisie was answering my question, even if she didn't know it.

How long are you staying?

I'm not staying. In fact, I never really arrived and I'm already halfway out the door.

"On what planet is a part in a movie a bad thing? Big or small?" Maisie yelled into the phone, pacing my living room. "His career has only existed for a hot minute, thanks to me. Anyone else would be thrilled to have this next step open up for them. Again, this step that opened up *thanks to me.*"

As she argued into the phone, growing more tense by the minute, I sat cross-legged in a blanket fort, sipping wine next to an uneaten meal, and fighting all my instincts. If I had my way, I would pull that phone out of her hands, tell the man on the other end that no one spoke to Maisie that way, then hang up right before smashing the device against the wall.

That last bit wouldn't accomplish much and was a little over the top, but at that point, it sure would have felt good.

The more she paced, the more foolish I felt. What had I expected would happen tonight? That I would make some goofy, childish gesture and she would abandon all the glitz and glam of the life she built for herself? On what planet was that an appropriate reaction to reuniting with an old friend with a ten-year-old phone? My life was slow and simple, and hers? Well, hers was on the opposite side of the country. I knew this was an inevitability, but had ignored the problem from the get go. I threw back the rest of my wine, then emptied the bottle into my glass.

Maisie stopped pacing and everything about her went slack. Her lips parted and her jaw dropped. Her shoulders slumped and her brows drew together. I wanted to pull her close, to wrap her up and make everything better. Whatever was happening, whatever she just heard, I wanted to keep her safe from it, just like I kept her safe when we were kids.

She hung up the phone and closed her eyes. Her lips quivered as she let out a long sigh. "That was my boss," she said without opening her eyes.

"I figured as much."

She bit her bottom lip. Then sucked both of them into her mouth. Then finally let out another long breath and opened her eyes. Tension thrummed along her body as she opened her mouth to say something that never made it past her throat.

I patted the pillow beside me and gestured to her glass. The situation was maddening, but I couldn't be mad at her. I'd asked her to stay and she did, even though she had to know it was going to make things difficult. What more could I want from her?

Ignoring the voice in my head that whispered *everything*, I said, "It's going to be okay." And it would be okay. No matter what happened next, I would do my best to make sure she was safe and happy.

"It's really not." Maisie stood, her shoulders slumped, sadness dripping from her posture. "I have to be back in LA by tomorrow or they're going to fire me."

TWENTY-THREE

Maisie

I HATED that I answered the phone. Not just because I interrupted a very important conversation with a man I respected more than anyone, but also because the answer to Caleb's question was becoming more and more clear by the second.

He wanted to know how much longer I would be staying and my boss wanted me back in Los Angeles three days ago. As I paced the living room with my phone pressed to my ear, my awareness split. One part of me paying attention to the reaming Mr. Lombardi was giving me while the other watched Caleb as he watched me from his place in the blanket fort.

A blanket fort. The man made me a blanket fort

and for as ridiculous as it sounded, the gesture couldn't have been more perfect. There wasn't a single other thing he could have done to say *I care about you, Maisie Brown. I see who you are, and I care.*

While I argued with my boss, Caleb downed a whole glass of wine, then poured himself another and started working on that, too. As Mr. Lombardi went to town making sure I knew just how irresponsible and unprofessional I was for going incommunicado on my own damn vacation, Caleb nodded as if he was coming to conclusions and answering his own set of questions in his head.

"Collin's lawyers are involved, Maisie. You hear me? His *lawyers.* He says you're in breach of contract."

"Breach of contract? For going on vacation?" But even as I put up a fight, I realized my error. Back when we first started our relationship, Collin had insisted on a clause to our contract, one that promised I wouldn't go more than three days without responding to his queries. At the time, I'd laughed off the clause. For one, Collin had seemed like a decent guy who wouldn't get that needy. And for two, when had I ever gone three days without checking my phone?

I ran a hand through my hair as the true weight of the situation settled onto my shoulders. "Shit."

A lawsuit. A frickin' *lawsuit.* Quicksand had crept

up to my neck while I lounged around watching TV, pretending to be a normal person.

Mr. Lombardi launched into another diatribe about my carelessness and how stupid he had been to put so much faith in me while I was young and under-qualified. He used more than a few choice words that spun in the pit of my stomach.

"Mr. Lombardi," I said when he took a breath, trying to sound stern and professional, not like my world was dropping out from under me. "You have no right to talk to me like that." I took a breath, fully intent on continuing, but he interrupted.

"I have every right to talk to you like that. The reputation of my agency is at stake and that means it's my name on the line. If we lose a client like Collin *fucking* West right after you launched his ugly ass to astronomic heights, I will make damn sure you never work in this town again. I. Will. Ruin. You."

He continued, and I was drunk enough, or angry enough, or off my guard enough to argue until he dropped a bomb on the conversation. "You will either be back in Los Angeles, behind your desk, licking West's ballsack if that's what it takes to calm this dipshit down, by tomorrow night, or you're fired." And with that, Jacob Lombardi ended the call, clearly not at all worried about the harassment case I could build against him off the strength of that last statement alone.

I closed my eyes, fighting an onslaught of tears and anxiety as I digested everything that happened, wishing I could go back in time, ignore my stupid phone, and answer Caleb's question.

How long are you staying?

Forever. I'm never leaving. You've always been my everything and now that I remember that, there's no reason for me to want anything else ever again.

Except stuff like that only happened in fairytales. In the real world, responsible adults needed to be able to support themselves and last I checked, there wasn't a whole lot of demand for talent agents in Key West.

I opened my eyes and found Caleb watching me. He had every right to yell. To get indignant and throw blame. I answered the phone when I shouldn't have, sending a message I had no intention of sending.

You mean less to me than my job.

Which wasn't true. He meant so much more to me than my job—and Shift was my entire life.

Instead of laying into me or asking me to leave, he patted the pillow beside him, offering the comfort of his strength and support when I wasn't sure I had earned it. "It's going to be okay," he said, and his words brought a ball of emotion up to catch in my throat.

When I explained the conversation, Caleb smiled sadly, then put down his glass of wine and crawled out of Fort Casie the Second, accidentally pulling the thing down around him as he miscalculated his size. "Guess we're not kids anymore," he said as he stared at the mess.

I shrugged, the weight of his words settling onto my shoulders. "Guess we're not."

I thought this was our goodbye. I expected him to send me on my merry way, silently cursing me for ruining the equilibrium of his life. But when he finally looked at me, there was something beautiful in his gaze. Something I wanted to fall into, to lose myself in, a forcefield to insulate us from the world.

Caleb reached for my hands, delicately twining his fingers through mine, then pulled me close. I pressed my head to his chest, and he held me tight without saying a word. The steady thrum of his heartbeat reached out to mine, a rhythmic reminder that he was flesh and blood and not some figment of my imagination.

This was Caleb Hutton. My best friend. My soulmate. My past colliding with my present and if I listened to what my heart was saying in response to his, then he was my future, too.

Tears burned in my eyes and I squeezed them shut, afraid that if I started crying, I would never stop. But my breath hitched, and my soul opened up, and before I could say anything about it, I was sobbing into Caleb's chest as he ran a soothing hand through my hair and whispered sweet words into my ear.

I wasn't even sure why I was crying. Was it because of what my boss said? Because I realized that my perfect life wasn't quite as perfect as I thought? Was I crying for the little girl I used to be? The one who never had a chance, but dug her heels in and made one for herself, despite what everyone said? The one who still hadn't taken a moment to slow down or breathe? Was I crying for my parents and the terrible life they lived? Was I crying for what Caleb and I could have been? What we were?

Or was I crying for all of it?

In Caleb's arms, I purged myself of a lifetime of ignored sorrow and piled up pain. When I finally regained control, he guided me over to the couch and presented me with a box of tissues.

"I'm so sorry," I murmured while I swiped at my eyes.

Caleb took my free hand. "Don't be. I understand. I'm here for you, if you want to talk."

"I don't even know where to begin. It's all so jumbled up inside." I dropped my head into my hand. "I guess I should start looking at flights if I'm going to be back in the office by tomorrow."

With a sigh, Caleb shifted in his seat. "You don't have to go back."

Hope flared to life and I glanced up, afraid I had misheard him. I wanted to stay. It just wasn't possible. "Jacob Lombardi doesn't make idle threats. If I want to keep my job, I have to go back."

"But, I guess what I'm saying is, do you even want to keep your job?" His low voice rumbled between us, his words both soothing the ache in my heart and jolting my anxiety back into action.

"What? Caleb. I wouldn't be able to find another agency willing to take a chance on me if I blow this."

"Maisie. You're not hearing me. I'm asking you to stay. Like, stay for good. Here, with me, in the Keys."

I blinked away my confusion. This was the first question he had asked me that I didn't have an immediate answer for. All the other ones had received an instant yes. But this one...

This one...

I wanted to say yes, but it was such a risk. Giving up my career after just a week...a wonderful week, yes, but still just a week. It reminded me of something my dad would do. The kind of rash decision that came with the last name of Brown.

"I want to stay with you, but..." I turned up my palms as my old self warred with my new self. "I have no way to support myself here."

My heart began to protest and excitement bloomed at the thought of moving back home to be with him.

The thought stunned me. When did I start thinking of the Keys as home instead of LA? I closed my eyes, trying to get a better sense of the feeling before it dissipated like a puff of dandelion in the wind...

"I know it's a lot," Caleb said. "It's a huge change. And I wouldn't ask you to even think about it if I didn't believe we were worth it." He shifted again, squeezing my hands in his. "What we have...it's worth fighting for. Tell me you don't feel it and I'll back off."

I met his eyes, my mind going into overdrive as I considered the ramifications of the choices in front of me. "Would you do it?" I asked. "If it were me, asking you to give up everything you had here to come to LA and be with me, would you?"

Caleb blinked and sat back a fraction of an inch. "I'd have to think about it. But I *would* think about it." He grabbed the back of my head and pressed his forehead to mine. "I don't want to lose you again."

Tears welled in my eyes as I digested both his hope and his sorrow and found them echoed inside me. "And I don't want to lose you." I pressed my lips to his, sobbing into his mouth as the impossibility of the situation came into focus. No matter what choice I made, it would be the wrong one.

And the right one.

"I need time to think about it." I ran my hands through his hair, gripping it in my fists as if I could physically hold us together. "And I think I need to do it alone. Because I can't think straight when you're around." I stood and gathered my things, then when it came time to leave, I couldn't.

"I love you, Maisie."

"I love you, too." I raised up on tiptoes to kiss him again, then left before I could talk myself out of it.

TWENTY-FOUR

Maisie

I LEFT Caleb's house and couldn't bring myself to head back to The Hut. So many good memories lived there, I wasn't prepared to face them. And so, with my eyes still swollen from tears, I plopped into the driver's seat of my rental and drove, not fully aware of where I was going until I arrived in front of my old house.

Thankfully, it was vacant, as nothing could have stopped me from getting out of my car. My feet moved on autopilot up the rickety old steps, the last one squealing in protest just as it had done a lifetime ago. The sound dredged up the sense of dread that used to wrap around my heart every time I came home. Grime covered the windows, but I peered inside to what used to be my living room.

My pulse pounded in my ears as echoes of my father's voice roared in my head. I straightened, hoping to silence the memories, but the dam had been broken and they rushed back in one disgusting mass. I remembered lying in bed, hunger gnawing at my bones and keeping me awake night after night while Mom and Dad fought. Their raised voices vibrating anxiety straight into my heart, so deep, it became a facet of my personality—meek, nervous, scared little Maisie.

Please, I would pray each night. *Take me away from here. Keep me safe. Make them stop fighting.*

Over and over, I murmured those words, pressing shaking hands against my ears, until eventually I drifted to sleep. The one bright spot in my days was Caleb. To my young eyes his blond hair shone like an angel's. His smile was always warm and the only time I felt safe was when he was around. But inevitably, he would have to leave my side because he and I lived in different worlds. Caleb didn't belong to me and as much as I wanted to belong to him, the terrible choices of my parents ensured that would never happen.

And now, all these years later, he was here, extending his hands and inviting me into his life. And he was just as warm and I felt just as safe, but how could I be sure those feelings weren't echoes of what I felt for him when I was young? How could I trust that any of this was real? I had only had him back for a week. I couldn't make a choice this big when I had nothing but intuition and a few wonderful days to base my decision on.

But you've leaned on your intuition before...

Yeah. And it let me down. I thought Collin West was a sure thing. And yes, he was, in a way. But he had since proved he wasn't the guy I thought he was. Instead of sweet and humble, his ego exploded almost as fast as he did. The man I thought would never take advantage of the strange clause he insisted be added to our contract was lawyering up and ruining my life.

So much for trusting my gut.

And what about my heart? What did it have to say?

I wandered around the rotting shack that used to be my home, my throat so tight it hurt to swallow. The stagnant air pressed in on me and I yearned for the breeze that would cool the sweat at my brow if I was on the beach at The Hut. But I hadn't gone there. Instead, I had come here, to this place that sat like poison in my soul, hunkered in the back of my mind like a great looming shadow over everything I ever accomplished.

No matter how much I ignored my past, it was always back there, reminding me that I would never be as good as the people around me.

And that was why I couldn't move back to the Keys.

If I wanted to truly close the door on who I used to be, I needed to get the hell out of there and never look back. And so, with tears streaming down my face, I sat down on that dilapidated porch, pulled out my phone, and started looking for flights.

TWENTY-FIVE

Caleb

AFTER A LONG AND very sleepless night, I spent a rough day out on the water. I just didn't have it in me to be Cap'n Caleb Hutton and for the first time in my career, the tourists in my care seemed less than enthusiastic about their adventure. My last tour ended at noon and I fought the urge to call Maisie for about an hour. She didn't need any more pressure riding on her than she already had. So I finally gave up and headed to The Hut to see my family, knowing I would drive myself crazy if I spent one more minute alone.

Both Wyatt and Lucas were in the office, hunched over the desk and studying a mess of papers, when I burst through the front door. They looked up when I stepped in, as strains of guitar music swooped into the hall from the kitchen, courtesy of Harlow and her never-ending font of creativity.

"Hey, Moose." Wyatt sat back in his chair and threaded his hands behind his head. "If only we knew you were coming, we would have made sure to stock the fridge. As it is, we only have enough food to feed a small army. Think you'll be able to make do?"

Last night's dinner still sat in my fridge, untouched. My appetite had left with Maisie. "Very funny," I shot back, then pulled out a chair and sat beside Lucas. "What are we working on?"

Luc made a face. "*We* are looking at some very important hotel documents."

"How very subtle of you." I leaned forward to quickly scan the papers, for no other reason than to piss off my oldest brother for being a dick.

Wyatt caught my eyes, aware of what I was doing and why. "We're going over estimates and projections for the next couple years." He beamed, very much the proud papa. "Things are looking good for The Hut. Better than they have in a long time."

"That's great." I bobbed my head and smiled wide, happy to finally see things looking easy for Wyatt. "Dad kicking the bucket keeps on being a good thing."

Silence fell on the room as we all searched for something to say. I was interrupting their workday, and they couldn't understand why I had appeared out of nowhere. I fidgeted with the hem of my shirt, looking for anything to talk about that might silence the constant buzzing background of worry shaking me apart at the seams. "Have you heard anything from Eli?"

Both Wyatt and Lucas shook their heads. "Nope," Wyatt said while Lucas murmured a low, "Un-uh."

"Yeah. Me neither. I wonder if we should call him or something. He's not one to go radio silent for so long." My attention wandered out the window behind Wyatt while thoughts of Maisie took over. What was she doing? Was she looking at flights? Had she already booked a flight?

Surely she would call me when she made a decision...

Surely she wouldn't disappear on me again...

Yanked out by the roots, leaving a wound in my life where she belonged...

"Caleb?" Wyatt leaned into view, snapping my attention back to the present. "Do you think there's something wrong with Eli?"

I glanced at my brothers, Wyatt looking concerned and Lucas beginning to look annoyed, and shook my head, slapping my hands on my knees as if I would stand at any moment. "What? Oh. No. I'm sure he's fine."

But I didn't stand because the thought of being alone was horrendous.

"All right," Lucas snapped, squaring his shoulders and lifting his chin. "There's obviously something on your mind. Stop beating around the bush and spit it out, Moose."

My brother was proof you could take the man out of the Marines, but you couldn't take the Marine out of the man. "All right, fine." I rolled my eyes dramatically and gave a wide grin to Wyatt, who loved getting under Lucas' skin almost as much as I did. "If you insist. Wow. Pushy much?"

Lucas glared and Wyatt laughed and I held up both my palms. "Honestly, I'm going a little crazy right now and would appreciate your advice, especially because you two seem to have things all locked up in the female department." I launched into my story of the last few days with Maisie, how intense the attraction was, how easy it had been to fall into old patterns. How what had once been a perfect friendship now came with intense chemistry. "I love her. I know it's crazy. I know it's too soon. I know I barely know the adult her, but..." I shrugged. "I love her."

"And she has to be back in LA by tonight." Wyatt leaned forward, folding his arms on the desk.

I nodded. "Or she'll lose her job."

"And where is she now?" Lucas asked.

"Thinking things through."

Luc frowned. "Thinking what through?"

"I asked her to stay," I said, as if it wasn't the most selfish thing I had ever done in all of my life. Maybe, if I pretended it was a perfectly normal thing for one adult to ask another, Lucas wouldn't notice.

No such luck.

His jaw dropped. "You asked her to stay?" he asked incredulously.

I leaned forward, elbows on knees as I stared at my hands. "There's so much to the story…"

"She's dedicated her life to that job."

"She has." I nodded my recognition of how hard Maisie worked to get to where she was. "But she's not happy."

"And you think she'd be happy here?" Lucas' question was genuine, holding zero judgement or sarcasm.

"She seems happy here," I replied. "She *says* she's happy here."

And, she had also seemed more and more stressed with each passing day. When I ran into her at her friend's bachelorette party, Maisie had a bright energy to her. She was bold and confident and set on her path.

Lately, that brightness had dimmed. I had assumed it was because of the pressures the people she worked with were piling onto her.

But what if she just wasn't suited for life in the Keys?

What if the slow, meandering pace I set was in direct opposition to her nature?

What if the stress I had seen growing in Maisie had more to do with the pressures *I* was putting on her? I frowned, then explained what I was thinking to my brothers.

"Cat told me she worked on Maisie the other day." Lucas held my gaze. "And that she couldn't believe how much tension she was holding onto, especially considering how happy she seemed when they first met."

What if that tension was because of me? "Why does it have to be so complicated?" I groaned, scrubbing my face with my hands, and looked to Wyatt.

"Love is not for the faint of heart." He gave me an empathetic smile and a faint shrug.

"So what should I do?"

"Fight for her. Love her. Support her."

Lucas nodded his agreement. "And if she chooses her life in Los Angeles, and you truly love her, you have to let her go. Don't make her split her heart in two."

And what about my heart? The thought of Maisie leaving again ripped open old wounds that had scarred over years ago. I had lost her once. Did I really have to go through losing her again?

The look on her face last night said everything. She had already made her decision, even if she hadn't accepted it yet. Maisie was leaving and I was going to have to find a way to be okay with that. Because I couldn't be selfish and keep her with me and I knew I couldn't go with her.

There was nothing in Los Angeles for me.

Except her.

And there was nothing in the Keys for her.

Except me.

The realization thickened my throat and I sank back into my chair, my gaze on my knees as I rubbed a hand along the back of my neck.

"I'm sorry, Caleb." Lucas' voice was full of understanding and that was almost too much for me. My hard-ass Marine brother never showed what he was feeling.

I stood, avoiding eye contact. "Yeah. It is what it is." I managed to smile. "Thanks for listening."

They both stood, murmuring platitudes I didn't listen to, and I raced out of The Hut because the walls were closing in and I needed open space and fresh air. I stopped on the porch, arrested by a memory of Maisie racing up the steps, her pigtails streaming behind her as one of those rare bursts of laughter chased her into the house.

With a deep inhale, I set my jaw, climbed into my car, and headed home.

TWENTY-SIX

Caleb

HER CHOICE WAS INEVITABLE. Even as I asked her to stay, I knew that Maisie would have to leave. Selling apartments, quitting jobs, moving across the country on a whim, those weren't things people did.

Our lives were like great wheels, perpetually rolling, building up momentum with each passing year. You couldn't just stop things from moving forward because you realized they weren't the way you wanted them to be. And even if you decided to try, the risk of getting squashed as it all rolled right over you was a very real thing.

I had been a fool to ask Maisie to stay. Our paths diverged years ago and no amount of wishing on my part could bring them back together. I should have let her go after her friend's wedding. And I should have let her go again the moment she got the call from her boss.

Each day she spent with me was delaying the inevitable. We'd been ignoring the wheel and here we were, about to be squashed.

When I came home from visiting my brothers at The Hut, Maisie was waiting on the porch, sitting on the top step, elbows on knees, gaze on her feet. Her hair was long and loose, billowing in the breeze off the water. When she looked up, her eyes were hidden behind dark sunglasses. She lifted them onto her head, revealing tear-stained cheeks and a red nose. She stood as I approached.

"Hey." She choked on the word and swallowed hard, wrapping her arms around her chest as if she were afraid to touch me.

I leaned on the handrail, one foot on the bottom step, and looked up at her. "Hey yourself."

"So...I came to say goodbye." Her gaze touched mine then dropped right back to her feet. Her bottom lip quivered and she wiped her nose with the back of her hand.

"I figured as much." I wanted to take the last few steps and wrap her in my arms, hold her close and never let her go, but my brother's advice whispered in my head. *And if she chooses her life in Los Angeles, and you truly love her, you have to let her go. Don't make her split her heart in two.*

I needed to touch her but if she felt the way I did whenever we got close, would that make it harder for her to say what she needed to say?

"Is there anything I can do?" I stepped closer despite myself. "Some way I can help?"

Maisie sucked in her lips and shook her head. "The flight is booked. I'm all packed. I'll land in Los Angeles around nine thirty PST, giving me enough time to be in the office before end of day." She gave a light shrug of her shoulders and finally met my eyes. "Caleb...I am so sorry..." Emotion swallowed the rest of the sentence and I took another step toward her.

"There's nothing to be sorry about." I took the last step and brushed a piece of hair out of her face. "It was silly of me to ask you to stay. Silly, and selfish, and I'm sorry I put that pressure on you. It wasn't fair of me."

She leaned into me and I wrapped an arm around her shoulder. "So now what?" she asked, sniffling.

"Well, you see, there's this crazy thing called the internet," I began. "I'm just now learning about it, but some people can hold it in the palm of their hands with this incredible device called a smartphone."

Maisie let out a little snort of a laugh and nuzzled in closer. "Very funny, Mr. Two Thousand and Four."

I fished in my pocket and pulled out the phone I

bought on my way home. "We don't have to end like we did the last time. I hear you can talk through video with these things. What's it called? Video phone? Video talk? Something ridiculous like that." I dropped her a wink. "And text, and email, and something called Facegram? Instabook? I already forgot, but the point is, basically we can stay connected even though our lives want to keep us apart."

She took the device from my hand, grinning through her sadness. "I can't believe you bought a phone. This thing is top of the line."

"The things you do for love," I said as if I had made a soul-crushing concession.

Maisie made a sound that was trying to be laughter but sounded a lot like tears. "Do you even know how to use this thing?" she asked as she spun it in her hands.

"No clue. But I'm sure I'll have plenty of practice figuring it out."

"You sure will," she replied as she programmed her information into my contacts. "Because I'll be emailing and texting and calling and *video-chatting* with you at least four times a day."

"Only four times?"

She gave me a watery smile and handed back the phone. "You always were everything I ever needed."

"You better remember that while you're rubbing elbows with the rich and famous."

She made a derisive sound. "You mean bending to the will of the pretentious and ridiculous."

"Same thing." I turned, pressing a finger to her chin and lifting her gaze to mine. "I love you, Maisie Brown. Always have. Always will."

Fresh tears glimmered in her eyes. "I love you, too." She bit her bottom lip and I pressed my forehead to hers, wiping away her tears with my thumbs.

We kissed and that wonderful moment of contact communicated all the things we couldn't. All the sorrow, all the hurt, all the confusion at having to say goodbye passed between us. Maisie pulled away. Tried to speak and couldn't. Ran her hand along the side of my convertible as she walked to her car with me trailing a few steps behind like a little lost puppy, then climbed into her rental and drove away.

And just like that, Maisie was gone.

Again.

TWENTY-SEVEN

Maisie

MY PLANT DIED. After walking away from Caleb, crying through the entire flight back to LA, and heading to my office with a throbbing headache and puffy eyes, finding those brown leaves draped over our picture was the final straw.

I expected more tears, but it seemed I was all cried out, so I just stared at it numbly for a long time until I heard someone behind me.

"Oh, thank God you're back." Brighton's voice held an undercurrent of something less than happy at my arrival and I let out a long sigh. I'd forgotten how tiring it was to live in a world where no one said what they were actually thinking.

"I don't think you mean that."

I didn't turn to face her, surprising myself with that burst of honesty. Maybe my feelings were still too raw. Or maybe I had gotten used to living without a filter around Caleb. Or maybe I was just tired of all the bullshit. Whatever it was, I'd have to learn how to put that filter back in place if I was going to survive the next couple of weeks.

Brighton gasped. "Whatever would make you say such a thing?"

I didn't have a showdown in me, and because I had to remember how to survive in LA-mode sooner rather than later, I faced my friend and lied through my teeth. "I have no idea. Forgive me? It's been a really long day."

"Oh, sweetie." She wrinkled her nose when she saw my swollen eyes and red nose. "What's wrong?"

If she had been paying attention, any attention at all, she would easily understand why I had been crying for the last twenty-four hours. The fact that she had to ask the question spoke volumes.

I was in love. I had been for all of my life. And instead of choosing him, I chose...this.

"I'm just worn out." I smoothed back my hair and blinked away the tears threatening to fall. "Didn't even stop at home, you know? Came straight here from the airport."

Brighton frowned as she took in my natural waves and makeup-less face. "You definitely look like you've been traveling. Come on. Let's find a bathroom. Once you clean up a little, you'll be feeling like yourself again in no time."

TURNED OUT, Collin's threat of suing me for breach of contract had been all for show. At least that was the story he tried to sell me once I was back at his beck and call. If I was to return to fighting in his corner again, we would have to be friends. And friends didn't sue each other.

"That crazy woman who took over for you while you were MIA?" He kicked his feet up onto my desk so I had to stare at the bottoms of his shoes. "She did everything but suck my dick to manipulate me into signing with her. Lawyering up was even her idea, though I don't think it turned out quite the way she hoped." He leaned forward. "I think she thought you'd end up fired, not back behind that desk," he clarified. "I'd watch your ass with that one."

Obviously, he meant Brighton and while I must have known that was what we were to each other on some level, having it put in my face was still unpleasant.

I gathered my hair over my shoulder—still wavy, thank you very much. It reminded me of how I felt with Caleb and I wasn't ready to give that up. As soon as Collin left my office, I snapped a smiling pic of myself with the crazy view through my windows as the backdrop and sent it to Caleb.

Miss you and that stupid fake accent of yours.

I sat back behind my desk and tried to focus on my work until my phone buzzed with a response.

Nice view, but mine's better.

A video came through of nothing but water and sky, then the view shifted to take in Caleb's smiling face. "Miss you, too, May-bell," he said with a whole lot of extra drawl, then winked.

I laughed out loud, then sat back in my chair, smiling, as tears formed in my eyes.

MY LIFE REMEMBERED ITS RHYTHM, even if I didn't. As days turned into weeks, things at Shift gathered momentum, adding more high performing clients to its roster—and none of them were mine. In the past, I'd have fought tooth and nail to represent the kind of talent we were bringing in, choosing to stay at the office until well after the stars blanketed the sky—even though the light pollution of the city hid them from view. That was, after all, the entire point of the couch nestled against the wall and the extra set of clothes and toiletries I kept at work. Sometimes I just didn't go home.

Instead, I set clear boundaries around my office hours, ensuring I left work no later than seven pm so I could be home for my evening call with Caleb. On Friday's I left at five, so he and I could cook dinner together, each of us working from the same recipe as we laughed over Skype, then comparing the outcomes. That had Caleb eating pretty late, but he swore he didn't mind. The rest of the week, we would watch some Netflix, hitting play at the same time, then sending goofy texts to each other throughout the evening. But a lot of the time, we just talked.

I told him about my days, not bothering to sugar-coat the challenges the way I used to, and he would tell me about his. We talked about the past and the present, but rarely the future, because neither of us liked what lay ahead. It was glorious to have him as a fulltime feature in my life, but Skype and text and poorly connected phone calls had nothing on leaning into him and hearing the breath in his lungs, his heart in his chest...to feeling the warmth of his skin, to falling into those magnificent eyes as they saw straight through to the core of me...

It had been a mistake to come home.

But staying would have been a mistake, too.

And between that rock and hard place, I was trying to carve out my existence, struggling to breathe as one pinned me against the other.

TWENTY-EIGHT

Caleb

IT WAS a sad day when hours out on the water couldn't lift my mood. Work had...happened. The excursion had been so uneventful, I couldn't even remember how things went. My tourists had been quiet and uninspired, because I had been withdrawn and uninspiring. Irritation gnawed at me when I disembarked, so I headed right back out onto the water to fish.

Fishing was my go-to. My ace in the hole. There wasn't a time in my life that I could remember a day spent with a line in the water *not* being good for my soul.

Except all I could hear was Maisie explaining

things from the fish's point of view. Her laughter echoed through my mind. Her smile. A flash of her hair as she ran through my living room, calling me a giant monster for manhandling fish. The memories brought a smile to my face and a heaviness to my heart.

I was happy to have Maisie in my life now. I really was. Talking over the phone was fine. And texts were fine. And cooking ridiculous meals over Skype was fine.

But those were a hollow substitute for the real thing. I wanted her back. I wanted to touch her. To smell her. To have her. I wanted to fall into bed with her at the end of each day, make love to her, and then wake up freezing because she spent the night hogging the covers.

And so, I reeled in my line, pulled up the anchor, and headed back toward land, unsatisfied with the ritual for the first time in my life.

AFTER MY NIGHTLY call with Maisie, I still had a decent case of the blues. Several lonely hours stretched ahead of me and I wasn't in the mood to spend them alone. I sent Eli a text, asking him what he was up to and he shot back two words.

busy tonight

Fine. Be a dick. It's not like you haven't been around for the last couple weeks or anything.

After a brief conversation with Wyatt, who was on his way to dinner with Kara, and then a call to Lucas, who was watching a movie with Cat, I hopped in the car and drove to The Hut. Mom would be there with Harlow and maybe, just maybe, the women in my family would have some advice for me —seeing as my brothers were seriously letting me down.

Only, Mom wasn't there.

"What do you mean she's on a date?" I asked Harlow, who sat on the front porch, her guitar at her side and her laptop open in front of her.

She gave me a withering look. "What exactly about that statement doesn't compute?"

"Just, I don't know." I shrugged. "I guess I'm having a hard time seeing her as, you know…"

"A woman? With needs and feelings?"

I sat down beside my sister. "Yeah. Kind of. I mean, I'm really happy for her."

"Sounds like it." Harlow rolled her eyes as she closed her laptop and set it aside. "You were the most vocal about Dad being an asshole. Why are you so bothered about Mom finding someone better than him?"

It was a good question, but my answer was just as

good. "That's the thing." I stared at my hands, then peeked at my sister. "What if he's not better?"

Harlow grimaced, acknowledging the point as valid. "She seems really happy, if that's any consolation."

It was, even though it couldn't quite soothe my fears of history repeating. Mom had a solid head on her shoulders. And if that failed her, she had me. If things with this guy got serious, and they looked like they were headed into familiar, craptastic waters, I would speak up. My mother would never have to live with a selfish, self-destructive asshole and his narcissistic choices again. Not while I was around.

My sister and I chatted, staying comfortably far away from any mention of Maisie. I asked her about her plans, because she didn't seem like she had any intention of moving back out of The Hut any time soon. Harlow had been living in Seattle when Dad passed, came home for his funeral, and never left. At twenty-three, she was the only one of us who never really found her path, even though she had more than a few open in front of her.

"Mom said I could stay as long as I wanted to. You know, just until I find my bearings. Get a grip on things. I've been writing non-stop. Might even finally finish a book."

"There's a first time for everything."

Harlow sighed wistfully, staring past me as if she could look back in time and count up the lost manuscripts littering her path. "I'd call you out for being a dick, but I earned that one. How many books *have* I never finished?"

"How does Lucas die in this one?" It was a long-standing joke in our family. Our sister loved finding new and imaginative ways to kill off our oldest brother.

She frowned. "I'll hurt you if you tell anyone this, but I stopped killing him in my books after what happened in Afghanistan. Just didn't seem funny anymore, you know?"

"Wow. Yeah. I get that. How come you still joke about it, though?"

"Oh, come on. You see how much he hates all the nicknames Wyatt gives him. Luc would like life to go on, as if he isn't our Bionic Man, slash Robocop, slash guy with metal in his backside. Could you imagine how he would react if I started treating him differently?"

Silence settled over us for a bit and I watched a fern rustling in a pot. In the distance, someone laughed, a reminder that we shared our family home with a host of other people.

"Have you heard from Eli recently?"

Harlow gave me the side-eye. "I have..."

"What's he been up to?" I turned to face her,

surprised by how relieved I was to know someone had been talking to him. "He's not mad at me, is he?"

"*Should* he be mad at you?" she replied with a quizzical tilt of her head and a strange gleam in her eyes.

"I don't think so, but he's kind of disappeared..." I let the statement trail off as Harlow refused to look at me, a tiny smile tugging at the corner of her mouth. I recognized her question for what it was. Deflection. "You know something, don't you?" I asked, sitting forward.

My sister mimed locking her lips and throwing away the key, the joy of having a secret dancing across her face.

That look could only mean one thing. "You don't just know something. You know something *juicy*, don't you?"

"It doesn't matter what I know, because I swore to Eli I would never tell. Now. Let's change the subject to something much more interesting."

I gave her a warning look, but Harlow continued as if she didn't see it.

"What's going on with you and Maisie?"

"I don't want to talk about it."

"Come on, Moose. We both know that's why you came here."

"Maybe I just needed a distraction."

Harlow called my bluff and gave her attention to her laptop. "If you say so."

I held my tongue as she started to open it up, but hurried forward as soon as her fingers hit the keys. Once she lost herself to her writing, that would be the end to any intelligent conversation as she fell into the world on her screen.

"Fine," I replied as her nails clacked against the first set of keys. "Maisie and I talk every day and I still miss her like hell."

With a triumphant look, Harlow closed her device. "See." She tapped the side of her head. "I knew you needed to vent."

I explained how things had been going since Maisie left. How nothing in my life felt as worthwhile as it did before her visit. "It's like the volume has been turned down. Food doesn't taste as good. The water doesn't sparkle enough. I can't even fish!"

Harlow dropped her jaw. "That *is* serious." The best part? She wasn't joking. She knew how much fishing meant to me. "So what are you going to do?"

An idea popped into my head. It was ridiculous, but the more I tried to ignore it, the more attention it demanded. "I don't know," I replied even as I found myself trying to untangle the intricacies of the fledgling plan.

"I don't believe you." Harlow narrowed her eyes.

"It looks a whole lot like you have something on your mind."

And just like that, the idea was fully formed and functional. What it lacked in intricacy, it made up for in fear and uncertainty. "What if I went to visit her?" I turned to my sister. "She came and spent a week with me. What's keeping me from going to spend a week with her?"

Except that Maisie had to work.

And she hadn't extended an invitation, so maybe she didn't want me there.

Maybe she was satisfied with all the space between us.

Or maybe it would be exactly what we needed to bring some joy back to our lives.

Maybe we needed more time together to really figure out what this was between us.

With Harlow's help, I brought the idea to life. I would surprise Maisie by showing up in Los Angeles. She could show me her world, the way I showed her mine. And maybe, with a little luck, we could find a way to bring those worlds together.

TWENTY-NINE

Maisie

IT HAD BEEN A DAY. From oversleeping to burning my breakfast and spilling my coffee. To terrible traffic and several near misses accident wise. From Brighton being rude, to Collin being an ass, and Lombardi making vague threats and insinuations about my general lack of usefulness, I was ready to go home and lose myself to a conversation with Caleb, maybe drink half a bottle of wine, and fall asleep seriously regretting my life choices.

Ever since I came home, all the shine of my life had worn off. The people around me seemed pretentious instead of polished. My work felt useless in the worst possible way. My apartment felt cold and impersonal.

And, given that my plant had died while I was in Florida and I never replaced it, that was all I had. Work. And people from work. That was the entirety of my life.

Before, that had felt like winning the world. Like I had everything I ever wanted, wrapped up in a beautiful package with a bow on top. After just a week with Caleb, it was like I finally thought to look inside the box and there I was, devastated to find it empty.

I checked the time. Eleven in the morning and I was ready to call it a day. I didn't know what to do with that thought, but I did know that I couldn't keep feeling this way. I wasn't happy and that wasn't okay. Something had to give, I just didn't know what. If it was eleven for me, it was two for Caleb. He was probably preparing to go back out on the water, drawling like a superstar for his boatload of tourists. The thought brought a smile to my face—maybe the first one of the day.

At two pm my time, I had a photoshoot with an up and coming actress. She was young and sweet and about four minutes into her career, and audiences were eating her up in the best possible way. I wanted to be excited for her, but my experience with Collin taught me that even the sweetest people could have monsters hiding inside them, just waiting for the right set of circumstances to arise and set them free. The photoshoot would take maybe half an hour at most, but I was looking forward to leaving the office for a breath of fresh air—even if that air was tainted by the scents of the city.

My phone buzzed like an angry hornet on my desk. I yanked it off the handset, and forced a smile. "Maisie Brown," I chirped, as sweet as honey, audibly eager to please. The best way out of a bad mood was to pretend you were in a good one. Fake it till you make it.

Movement in the doorway caught my attention as Collin West started barking about the newest worst thing that ever happened to him since becoming a household name. I glanced up and nearly dropped the phone as my forced smile blossomed into a full blown, cheek cracking, grin of epic proportions.

There, leaning in the doorway of my office in Los-Freaking-Angeles, was none other than my heart's truest desire. He looked magnificent. A white shirt gleaming against tanned skin. Strong build commanding attention even as his casual demeanor suggested he didn't care what anyone thought about him. His relaxed confidence looking so out of place—and so damn appealing—in this office built on people's need for external validation.

"Caleb?"

Collin made an offended sound and started to say something as I stood, lowering the phone because in that moment I couldn't care less about what that red-headed ass had to say.

Caleb held out his hands. "There's the face I've been needing to see."

I brought the phone to my ear, told Collin I'd have to call him back, then hung up and sprinted across my office and into Caleb's arms. "Oh my God," I murmured into his chest, drinking in his scent, his warmth, just...him. "I am so happy to see you." The words felt hollow and inadequate. *Happy* was too small to describe how it felt to be with him again. His presence soothed an ache in my soul, a missing piece fitting back into place, calming a constant buzzing pain I had only been barely aware of.

"The feeling is mutual, May-bell," he drawled into my hair. "I tried to be decent and stay at the hotel instead of bothering you at work, but, turns out I'm greedy."

I stepped out of his arms, catching a few curious glances from coworkers as I pulled him into my office. "Why didn't you tell me you were coming?"

Caleb took in the view from my windows, nodding his appreciation. "You dropped into my life unannounced and made everything better. The least I could do is try and return the favor." He pointed at the window. "Much better in person, by the way."

I took his hand in mine and drew him close. "I

couldn't agree more." And as I stared into his eyes, the terrible, no good, very bad day became my favorite day this month.

Reversals of fortune, baby. Still rockin' my world.

A knock at the door caught my attention and I moved away from Caleb as Brighton stepped in. "I thought that was you," she said to him. "How are you, picture frame boy?"

He draped an arm around my shoulder and pulled me close. "Better now than I was."

"Why didn't you tell me he was coming in?" Brighton glanced over her shoulder and lowered her voice. "Trying to keep him a secret from Lombardi? I mean, I would. All he needs is a *reason* to explain why you've been so...you know...I guess I wouldn't quite say lazy..." She gave a light shrug of her shoulder. "But you know what I mean. If Lombardi could pin your change of attitude on this guy? It would give him all the ammunition he needed."

Brighton sounded just a little too pleased with the thought of Lombardi finding some ammunition.

Caleb turned to me with questions dancing all over his face. "Is there some kind of problem?"

Brighton put a hand to her heart. "Look at you, ready to jump in and protect her from her big bad boss. Aren't you just the sweetest?" She smiled just a little too wide. "We have to have dinner. The four of us.

Sawyer would be beside himself if he missed the chance to finally meet his best man." She grinned even wider. "Tonight? Say, eight o'clock? I'll leave work a little early and we can meet at Domingo's."

The last thing I wanted to do was share my first night with Caleb in Los Angeles with Brighton and Sawyer. "Honestly, Bri..."

"Oh, come on, Maisie. You have been zero fun since you came home. Don't say no." She turned her full attention to Caleb, and I recognized her wheeling and dealing face. She was working him like a client she wanted to make feel spectacular so she could attach to his stardom and catch a ride on his trajectory. I'd done it myself plenty of times, and for the first time, I was completely and utterly turned off by it. Before I knew what was happening, we had plans to meet at Domingo's for dinner that night, and Brighton sauntered out of the office, looking overly pleased with herself.

"You didn't have to say yes, you know." I grimaced, less than pleased with sharing Caleb with Brighton— especially after everything I learned about her behavior with Collin.

"The way I see it, the sooner we satisfy her, the sooner I have you all to myself." He leaned close to whisper in my ear. "And once I get you alone, the chances of you ever being seen again are slim." His proximity had butterflies shimmying to life in my stomach, stretching their glorious wings after a forced hibernation.

"How long are you here?" I asked, trying to bring the conversation back to something more appropriate. I was at work, after all. And Caleb's good looks and sudden appearance was stirring up quite a tornado of curiosity.

He shrugged. "A week. Week and a half. Got all my tours shut down and I am officially yours for the next seven to ten days." He lowered himself onto the couch, rested his ankle on his knee and threw an arm up on the back. "So, this is where the magic happens, huh?"

"This is it." I gestured around the space, trying to imagine it through his eyes. What did he see? The glitz and glam that I used to love? Or the pretentious affectations I was starting to loathe?

His gaze fell on the picture of us, still in its place of honor on my shelf. "My God. Look at us." He picked up the frame and ran a finger down the glass. "I loved you then, you know. You can see it all over my face. I just didn't know what it meant yet."

I studied the picture as if the answers to everything were hidden inside our four-hundred-watt smiles and dirt-streaked faces. "And what does it mean?"

"I don't know. Maybe it means I move out here to be with you." He grinned like it was the best idea he'd ever had. "Surely there's a place for Cap'n Caleb Hutton in the great state of California."

Judging by the quizzical glances from my coworkers, I'd say there were about fifteen people willing to strap their names to his and help him find that place. He had the looks. And the charisma. Maybe our paths crossed to bring him here, where he'd be discovered and start his career as the next McConaughey.

"There's always a place for you here." I pressed a hand to my heart.

Caleb turned, giving me a wounded look. "Only there?" he asked, his eyes glinting devilishly.

I laughed. A real, genuine burst of laughter that only served to remind me that I hadn't been doing a lot of that lately.

***

CALEB CAME with me to the photoshoot, still garnering a whole lot of attention that didn't seem to matter to him in the least. My sweet, budding starlet had a minor breakdown when the photographer asked her to pose with a snake...and while I understood her trepidation, I also was afraid I saw the first glimpses of who she would be when she grew into her star power.

I hoped I was wrong. I hoped I was just jaded after

my experiences with Collin. And Brighton. And, Mr. Lombardi, too.

As the snake was removed from set and the girl calmed down, I chastised myself for judging her too harshly. I just hadn't been myself lately and it was showing up in strange ways. From across the room, Caleb caught my eyes and grinned in that way of his, scattering all those thoughts to the wind.

THIRTY

Caleb

MAISIE DIDN'T GO BACK to work after the photo-shoot. I'd been prepared to return to my hotel and give her space to do what she needed to do. I was, after all, fully aware I had appeared right in the middle of her workday. Instead, she made a call and some vague excuses, then after a stop at the hotel to collect my things and check me out, took me to her place.

"What were you thinking?" she asked over the roof of her car, her eyes narrowing in that way I found so adorable. "A hotel? Really?"

I gathered my bag from the trunk, pushing the lid closed. "Didn't want to presume, especially because I was dropping in on you all unexpected, like. Maybe you're secretly a hoarder and needed some time to clean up before I could see how dirty you really are."

"Oh, don't you worry. You'll be seeing a very dirty side of me." She tried to give me a seductive look, but a smile broke across her face, totally ruining the effect. "I'm sorry." She laughed lightly as she threaded her arm through mine. "I don't think I've stopped grinning since you showed up."

As I stepped into Maisie's apartment, it quickly became clear that she was the exact opposite of a hoarder—whatever that was. Her furniture was new and modern and barely looked used. A few pieces of tasteful artwork adorned the walls, though there wasn't a single piece of personal anything to be seen. Anywhere. All the surfaces were clean and void of ornamentation.

Lacking the bold, bright color that had become a staple of Maisie's personality, her place felt...sterile.

I wandered through the spacious living room, in search of evidence that the woman I loved existed here. "This is nice."

"Don't lie," she called from the entry as she paused to step out of her heels. "You hate it." She walked into the room, her shoes dangling from her hands, looking every bit as beautiful as I remembered.

"Hate is a strong word, May-bell." I gestured

around the space. "It's lovely. There's just not a whole lot of you in here."

She looked around, her brow furrowed as if she was seeing everything for the very first time. "I'm really not home all that much," she replied with a shrug. "If I'm not at work, I'm probably asleep."

"You're not at work *or* asleep now." I held out my arms, fully aware that I was the reason she was home in the middle of the day...and desperately hoping it wasn't a bad thing. "Yet here we are."

"You're right. I'm not at work or asleep." Maisie took my hand and led me out of the living room, her hips swaying as her bare feet padded down the hallway. "But we are headed to the bedroom."

AND IN THE bedroom we stayed until it was time to get ready to meet her friends for dinner. While we were lounging around, naked and content in her bed, a text came in from Brighton, explaining that the plans had changed and we should "dress for the occasion."

"What's that mean?" I asked. "Dress for the occasion?" Thankfully, I had packed some nice clothes, intending to make the most of my time here. Let's be real. Thankfully *Harlow* suggested I pack some nice clothes, in case something came up that needed more than cargo shorts and a T-shirt.

Maisie shrugged. "Could mean any number of things with Brighton at the wheel. But, she's excited, so prepare yourself for something big."

"Well, that is all that matters, isn't it? Brighton's excited so all is right with the world." I pulled her back into my arms, nuzzling my face into her hair and groping one spectacular breast.

She giggled, then twisted to meet my eyes. "What matters is that I'm with you. The rest is just noise."

"I couldn't agree more." I kissed her forehead, the tip of her nose, the corner of her mouth. "The rest is just noise." And then I kissed her fully, our tongues tracing lazy circles around each other while the world moved on without us.

After a shower, Maisie disappeared into her bedroom and emerged wearing a little black dress that dipped low in front, highlighting both her fabulous legs and outstanding breasts. "That dress should be illegal," I said as I drank her in. "Wait. No. You wearing that dress should be illegal." I grabbed her waist and pulled her close. "Promise me you'll never take it off."

"Never?" She gave a little pout. "But I thought it would look extra good on my floor. Tonight."

"You're right. As always. Forget everything I just

said. That dress. On that floor. As soon as we get home."

While I dressed, Maisie worked magic on her hair and makeup and when she came out of the bathroom, she managed to look like my Key West Maisie dressed in her LA clothes. The effect was particularly stunning.

"You are a sight to behold, you know that?"

"No. But I sure like hearing you say it."

THIRTY-ONE

Caleb

BRIGHTON AND SAWYER were so excited about their surprise that they didn't want to spoil it by giving us the address for wherever we were going. So, they planned to pick us up outside Maisie's apartment, which they did in an older Toyota Prius. When I turned to Maisie with a question on my face she whispered, "Sawyer thinks those cars are ironic." And with that cryptic statement, the happy couple was out of the vehicle, engulfing us in hugs, energy, and excitement.

Once I managed to squeeze myself into the backseat with Maisie—wondering if the design team ever expected someone my height to fit back there—we got under way.

"So..." Maisie said to her friend as she took my hand, running a finger along my knuckle. "Are you going to tell us where we're going?"

Brighton turned in her seat, looking oddly plastic with her perfect hair and makeup. "You aren't going to believe it." She sounded so enthusiastic about surprising us with a special evening that I felt bad for judging her so harshly. The woman seemed sweet enough, even though something about her grated against my nerves.

"Probably not," Maisie replied, "but you should tell me anyway. You know I hate surprises."

"We pulled some strings, called a few people, sold our souls and..." Brighton glanced at Sawyer who grinned his ironic little head off. "We're going to Providence."

Maisie's jaw dropped. "Providence?"

Brighton nodded vigorously. "Can you believe it? And we went ahead and ordered four of the Chef's Tasting Menus and told them to let him go wild."

"What's a tasting menu?" I asked, genuinely intrigued by her enthusiasm.

Both Sawyer and Brighton let out a snort of laughter that managed to sound downright condescending. "Isn't that cute?" Brighton asked, before turning to Maisie. "He's never heard of a tasting menu.

I'm so used to living here, I forget what it must be like for everyone else."

Maisie gave my hand a squeeze. "Not everyone is quite as blessed as you, Brighton." I heard the underlying threat in her voice. A warning to her friend to play nice and stop trying to make herself feel big by making me feel small.

What Maisie didn't understand was that I couldn't care less what either person in the front seat thought of me. In fact, until quite recently, I couldn't care less what anyone outside my family thought of me. The only non-Hutton with an opinion that mattered was Maisie—and she mattered so much she might as well already be family.

That thought caught my attention.

...might as well already be family.

...already...

The fact that my mind chose to use that word suggested that somewhere, I had plans for her to become family in the future. That time just needed to pass to make it true.

I refocused on the conversation, hoping my face didn't betray the whirlwind of thoughts in my head. "Whatever it is, it sounds like I'm in for an adventure."

"That's the spirit," Brighton crowed, as if she was cheering on a kid at a soccer game.

Beside me, Maisie tensed, but I swung an arm up

on the back of the seat, settled in as best I could, and gave her a smile. Her friends could say or do whatever they wanted and all that mattered was that I was finally with her. "The rest is just noise," I whispered when she turned to me, appalled by Brighton's behavior.

Maisie grimaced and bit her tongue, but something told me it wouldn't take but one more thinly veiled dig at my lack of worldly experiences and she would pounce on her friends, claws out. She quietly explained what a tasting menu was—a collection of several dishes in small portions, served by a restaurant as a single meal—and that Providence was unbelievably expensive. Worry creased her brow, and I made sure to let her know that money was no issue, while also starting to wonder what kind of people her friends were. Who would go so far as to pull strings to make reservations at a restaurant sporting that many dollar signs on the menu without being sure everyone had sufficient dollars signs to waste on a meal?

Thankfully, we made it to our destination without issue and sat down for a dining experience like no other. The food was exceptionally good, even if the company continued to be lackluster. Brighton bragged about stealing a client from a co-worker, setting her colleague up to fail, then swooping in to save the day when things went bad, and signing the client for herself. She laughed as if it were all a great joke, unaware of Maisie's scowl and my frown. How could she find any of that funny? Or feel comfortable enough to brag about it?

Somewhere between one of the many courses, Sawyer lifted his wineglass. "I'm very glad to finally learn more about my best man. And go figure, he turns out to be one of the coolest people I've ever met. Like, I can only imagine how out of your element you feel right now, and you can barely even tell how out of place you are. I'm glad to know you, Caleb, especially considering what a great story it is...some random fisherman being my best man, then me taking him to dinner at a place like Providence, no less." He threw back his drink, like nothing was amiss.

Maisie lowered her glass, her smile disintegrating. "Caleb isn't some random fisherman."

I placed a hand on her knee under the table and smiled at Sawyer. "Life certainly has a way, doesn't it?" I took a drink and settled back in my seat. "I never thought I'd be happy to spend three hundred and fifty dollars on a meal and be mildly insulted by someone who thinks driving a Prius is ironic. But hey. Here I am. Happy as can be." I grinned at a shocked Sawyer who burst out laughing.

"I like this guy." He pointed at me, sharing a look of surprise with Maisie. "A lot."

"I do, too," she replied, before turning to me, her eyes searching mine as she tried desperately to apologize for her friends' behavior without saying anything out loud. When the meal was over, Maisie and I bid farewell to the dynamic duo, opting to walk around Melrose Avenue for a bit before catching an Uber back to her place.

As soon as they were out of sight, she tugged on my arm, stopping our stroll. "I am so sorry for all that. For them talking down to you. For them assuming you had that kind of money just laying around..." She glanced at me, uncertainty lacing her eyes. "If you *don't* have that kind of money laying around..."

I wrapped an arm around her shoulder and pulled her close. "I'm fine, May-bell. If the cost had been a problem, I would have ordered anything else. But thank you for worrying about me."

We walked a few steps in silence as night fell around us. The rush of cars down the street kept us company, and I snuck a glance at her profile. She chewed her lip, looking pensive, more like the little girl who needed me to save her from lunchroom bullies than the confident woman who fought back against a drunk the night we reconnected.

"That story Brighton told?" Maisie began, her gaze on her feet as her heels clicked across the pavement. "About stealing a client right out from under a colleague's nose? She tried to do it to me. In fact, that was the whole reason work blew up in my face while I was in Florida." Maisie shared a story her client shared with her as we strolled down the street, waiting for our Uber.

"Sounds like she's not your people." I stopped walking, taking her shoulders in my hands and turning her to face me because I needed to see her reaction and know that she understood how far above Brighton she was.

Maisie's eyes bounced across my face, a sad smile pulling at her mouth. "On some level I already knew that. You know the old saying, keep your friends close and your enemies closer. I knew that's what was happening. It just hurts to finally have proof of what I really am to her. Of who she really is."

Our ride arrived, the conversation moved on, and the mood changed dramatically as my hand found its way to her knee, then went on a journey of exploration under her skirt. We barely made it out of the car and into her apartment before we stripped each other bare. In a tangle of tongues and teeth and need and desire, we found our way back to her bedroom, setting the place on fire as we went.

"You were right," I said as she unzipped her dress. "That thing looks much better on the floor."

Maisie giggled and helped me out of my clothes,

making me groan with need when she wrapped her hand around my cock.

We didn't just make love, we made promises.

We didn't have to say anything, because somehow, our bodies communicated everything.

Our joy at being reunited...

The cruelty of fate that had us so tangled up, but living so far apart...

The sheer gratification that we were together and the complete and utter tragedy that we would be separated again in a matter of days...

Sweat beaded at our temples and trailed down our spines. This was the purest embodiment of a love that had come pre-installed for us, a truth from childhood we were just now understanding. We were made for each other, and with each thrust of my hips and every bounce of her breasts, we reaffirmed that fact, entwining our souls into this moment.

It was a beautiful, terrible thing, our connection. And I was going to cram as much of her into my system as I could before I had to learn how to breathe without her again.

The next day, I woke before Maisie, thanks to my internal clock still being set to east coast time. When she finally stumbled out of her bedroom, looking sexy and bedraggled and every bit of what I had been missing in my life for the last couple weeks, something clicked into place for me.

I sat with her while she inhaled her coffee, then watched in amusement as she buzzed through her morning. As she chattered away, I found myself daydreaming about life with her. Would this be a typical part of our morning, if we lived together? Me sitting quietly as she launched herself into her day, the human embodiment of energy and excitement.

"I hate that I have to work," she said as she finally came to a stop in front of me.

"Your life can't come to a screeching halt just because I'm here."

"Yeah. Well. It should." She kissed me, then kissed me again, then headed out the door.

THIRTY-TWO

Maisie

THE NEXT COUPLE days were equally wonderful and terrible. Coming home every night to Caleb was a blessing, but having the veil lifted from my eyes regarding Brighton jarred me. To make matters worse, now that I'd stopped fooling myself about her, I saw everything about my life differently, too. From the moment I graduated college, I had set out with the dream of helping people, following a winding path with unexpected turns that led me to my job at Shift. For years, I let myself believe that fate had brought me there, that while I wasn't helping people in the ways I imagined when I was younger, what I had was better. I was making dreams come true.

It wasn't better. Not at all.

It was a shallow excuse for the service I felt so called to provide. And for so many of my clients, the dreams I prided myself on helping come true eventually shifted into nightmares. Their circumstances changing so slowly they didn't notice until things had gone too far. Ever since dinner with Brighton and Sawyer, it became more and more clear that wolves and jackals surrounded me. Predators who were happy to take what they could from people, then eek out another percent or two of profit before the stars imploded in a rush of self-destructive energy.

I wasn't beneficial. Not in the ways I wanted to be. In fact, I was a commodity myself, a resource for Mr. Lombardi to use until I was no longer profitable...a state he seemed to think was fast approaching.

"Leaving already?" he asked from the doorway as I shut down my computer and gathered my things at the end of a very long day. His nonchalant tone dripped accusation.

I squared my shoulders and lifted my chin. Everyone at Shift prided themselves on the insane hours we were willing to work—and any other week, I'd be right there with them. But I only had a few more days left with Caleb and I intended to spend as much time with him as I could. "It's after five," I replied, as if that meant anything at all.

Lombardi looked unimpressed and took a step into my office. "I didn't see anyone else packing up for the day on my way over here. In fact, it seemed like most of my employees were gearing up for another couple hours of hustling."

Undeterred, I smoothed my skirt. "I have plans this evening..."

"And last evening. And tomorrow, I'm sure. You've made it pretty clear that your priorities are shifting, Ms. Brown." I hadn't been 'Ms. Brown' in a long time. Lombardi always called me by my first name. "You left part of yourself in Florida" he continued. "It's past time you found a way to bring her back."

I saw the point he was trying to make, and I knew he was referring to the part of me that was willing to stay at work all night if need be, the part ready to sacrifice all other aspects of her personal life to better serve the needs of the agency.

The thing was, he was right, though not in the way he intended. I did leave part of myself in Florida—my heart and soul, in the capable hands of Caleb Hutton. The only person in the world who knew all of me, who understood me, and didn't need me to sacrifice anything to prove my worth to him. When our paths crossed in that tiki bar on the coast, I reconnected with myself, with the parts of me that mattered, the bits and pieces I had ignored over the years because I deemed them irrelevant.

They weren't irrelevant, though. Even if they didn't fit into this perfect little box of how I wanted *successful* to look, they were the most important parts of who I was, buried beneath a veneer of designer clothes and meaningless connections.

Lombardi was still talking, continuing to insinuate my fall from grace was eminent as I lost my edge. He buried digs at my self-worth inside fake concern for my well-being, then full on threatened my job if I didn't rediscover my control and return to the straight and narrow.

"There's no room for mediocrity at Shift, Ms. Brown. Whatever you're going through, get through it. Pick yourself up. Dust yourself off. And get back on track."

His words hit me hard, though again, not in the way he meant them to. I *was* off track. Everything I had built for myself was like a funhouse mirror view of what I wanted to do and who I wanted to be.

Wrong side of the country.

Wrong people surrounding me.

Wrong apartment.

Wrong. Wrong. Wrong.

The only thing right about my life was waiting for me back home...and the crazy thing was, when I thought about home, my mind went straight to Key West.

"You're right, Mr. Lombardi." I smiled brightly as my thoughts came more clearly into focus. "It's time I stopped messing around and got my life back in order." There was nothing fake or forced about my expression. I was genuinely pleased by what I was about to say, which in itself felt unnatural. How many times had I put on a pleasant face for people when I felt anything but? How many times had I done it...and not even realized I was doing it?

"Good." He gave a curt nod and a satisfied smile. "I'm glad to hear that. It's hard to watch someone as talented as you self-destruct."

"Well, then you'll be happy to hear that I quit. Consider this my two-week notice." As his jaw dropped, I made my way out from behind my desk, grabbed the picture of Caleb and me off the bookshelf, and left.

Caleb would ask me to move back to Key West before he left, I was sure of it. Like me, he was relentless in going after what he wanted, only he took a more relaxed approach than I did. But because I knew that about him, I knew he wouldn't leave without trying one more time to keep us together. And this time, when he asked me to come home with him, I would say yes.

Caleb

AS THE DAY I would have to leave Maisie and head back home fast approached, I came to several conclusions.

One, I hated it in Los Angeles.

Two, I couldn't face life without Maisie.

Three, I was willing to put up with a little of what I hated in exchange for a lot of what I loved.

And so, after Maisie left for work that morning, I spent the day perusing apartments and looking for jobs. Nothing leapt out at me as a career I could see myself in long-term, but I had a list of bad ideas that might grow into the one good one that brought everything together. And that was a start, which was more than I had a few hours ago.

I wasn't going back to Florida. We wouldn't have to learn how to breathe without each other because I would be staying. Indefinitely. No more shallow breaths. We would be swimming in oxygen. That night, when she got home from work, we would have a reason to celebrate.

Using all of my newfound cooking skills, I made us a spaghetti dinner with homemade marinara, complete with a salad, garlic toast, wine, and candles on every surface. Maisie's schedule had become fairly predictable, so when she walked through the front door, wearing a surprised look on her face, dinner was on the table, the candles were lit, and I slipped a wine-glass into her hand as I led her to her chair.

I cupped her face between my hands and kissed her. "Welcome home, beautiful." As her questioning eyes locked onto mine, I realized this would be part of our new normal once everything was said and done. And that soothed the uncertainty of moving to a city that didn't suit me.

"What's all this about?" Maisie asked, looking shell-shocked as she clutched what looked like a picture to her chest.

"We have reason to celebrate." I took my seat beside her, trying to untangle the look on her face. She seemed nervous. And keyed up. Oscillating between a smile and what might be panic, her expressions changed faster than I could keep up.

"We do," she replied with a bob of her head. Her response was a statement, not a question, and that put me off my guard. How did she know we were cele-brating tonight?

I had intended to make it through dinner before I clued her in on how I spent my day, but considering her strange reaction, I decided to jump right in. "I've been doing a lot of thinking and I'm not ready to say goodbye to you again."

"That's funny," she replied. "I'm feeling very much the same way." Her smile had an expectancy about it, which only served to further throw me off my game.

"So...I've decided to move to Los Angeles."

Her reply nearly overlapped my statement. "Yes, I'd love to." As soon as the words were out of her mouth, her brow furrowed and she tilted her head. "Wait, what did you say?"

I slid off my chair and kneeled at her feet. "I can't leave you again, Maisie. And I can't keep asking you to give up your life so we can be together. Having to go home has been on my mind from the minute I got here, and I just can't do it. I can't. I spent the day looking at apartments and brainstorming ways I can make a living out here." I pulled my phone out of my pocket and showed her the list. "I don't exactly have the answer yet, but we're smart people...we can make this work."

Maisie laughed lightly, barely giving my phone a glance. "I thought you were going to ask me to move back to Florida with you."

"I couldn't ask you that. Not again. That would be too selfish..." Her words sank in, with her response to my revelation chasing behind like a puppy bounding through a field. I told her I was moving to LA and she replied with *I'd love to*. "Wait." I straightened and stared down at her, blinking as if my vision was the reason things weren't quite computing. "You thought I was going to ask you to move back home with me. And you said yes?"

"I quit my job today." Laughter tinged her words and happiness danced through her eyes.

I dropped into my chair, certain I had misheard her. "You did what?" Now I was the one looking shell-shocked, because that was exactly how I felt.

"I quit my job, Caleb. Having you here has been such a wakeup call. This isn't the life I want." Maisie shrugged. "It's like this apartment. All perfectly fine and expensive and exactly what the rest of the world would consider a dream come true, but it doesn't suit me. You suit me." She dipped her chin toward her shoulder. "I'm not exactly sure what happens after I move home with you, but I'm sure the rest will fall into place, as long as you'll have me."

Happiness spread through my veins like fire devouring gasoline. "You quit your job?" I stood, pulling her out of her chair right along with me. "You actually quit your job?"

She held out the framed picture of the two of us that had been clutched in her hands since she walked in. "I took the one thing that mattered to me and walked out the door. This picture had been pointing to the truth all along. Look around you, Caleb. Of all the things in my home and office, the only thing that ever mattered was you. I'll have to tie up some loose ends with my clients, of course. But...yeah." She let out a short breath. "I'm all yours if you'll have me."

"Oh, I'll have you, all right. Again and again. Over and over."

For the rest of my life, if I had my way...

THIRTY-THREE

Maisie

IN A WAY, Caleb's decision to make the move to Los Angeles was the final straw in my decision to move to Key West. Sure, I had already put in my two weeks' notice, but one frantic call to Lombardi would have reversed that in a heartbeat. He was screwed without me, and we both knew it.

It was Caleb's selflessness that solidified things. He didn't belong in Los Angeles, but he was willing to drop everything just so we didn't have to say goodbye.

For one, I couldn't let him do that.

And for two, I didn't belong in Los Angeles either.

I belonged with him.

We decided to skip all the usual relationship stepping stones and move in together instead of me finding my own place to live. On one hand, we knew it was fast, but on the other, we had some time to make up for. Besides, there was no denying what we had. He and I were designed to be together, our paths diverging long enough to teach us important lessons about who we were and what we wanted, then reconnecting at the perfect moment.

Over the next couple days, he helped me box up my things as we decided what would make the trip and what I needed to sell. Not much was coming with me because I hadn't accumulated much that mattered.

"I have enough savings to support me while I figure out how to make money," I said one night over dinner—Chinese takeout, a treat I very rarely allowed myself.

"Maybe you can start an agency of your own," Caleb suggested around a mouthful of moo shu pork. "You've got the drive. And the talent. You'd be a great business owner."

"I'm not sure Key West is the best location for that. Miami, maybe. But the Keys?" I shrugged. "Besides, I'm not sure this is really my calling. I'd like to find something better, you know? I set out with the great idea of helping people and I still feel that purpose inside me, looking for a way out. I really want to find a way to make life better for the people who need it most."

What we were doing was crazy. We knew that. Me, quitting a job so many people would kill for without another prospect on the horizon. Him, moving a woman he technically just met into his home. But no one made it big on safe bets and sure things. We didn't know how it was going to work out, just that it would.

Over the course of the next few days, I sat down with my clients and explained what was happening. Most of them took it in stride, wishing me well while they were already figuring out their next move. My little budding starlet actually cried when she thanked me for everything I had done for her, and swore she would find a way to make it up to me. I saved Collin for last and his reaction wasn't at all what I expected.

He perched on the edge of the couch in my office, his elbows on his knees and his gaze on the floor. "Is this because of me?" His voice was solemn and I saw a glimpse of the quiet man who first walked into Paradigm Shift Talent Agency, looking like he'd just won the lottery.

"Honestly? A little. But even more honestly, not at all." I explained my change of heart regarding the industry as a whole, keeping everything at a super high level so as not to drag anyone's name through the mud. "And...I fell in love," I added, once it was all said and done. "Which just made me realize all the more how... hollow...all this was."

Collin bobbed his head. "I've been thinking along similar lines myself. When that *friend* of yours"—he glanced up as he made air quotes —"got me all spun up about you taking some personal time, I had to take a long hard look at myself. I mean, you got me a part in a movie for God's sake. Me. In a movie. The kid who grew up bullied for his hair and his music and all the things that made him different, was gonna be on the big screen and somehow, that wasn't good enough. That's not me. Or at least it wasn't."

Lost in the nostalgia of those first few days with Collin, I stared at the man in front of me. It was one of those times when you knew, you really, really *knew* you had something special on your hands. "You're right, it wasn't. The man who signed with me was completely flabbergasted at what was happening to him. God, your energy was so inspiring."

"And I lost that. Quickly." He dragged his gaze off the floor to meet mine. "I'm not proud of it."

"We all make mistakes, Collin. If letting the glitz and chaos of being suddenly famous go to your head is the worst thing you do, I still think you're gonna be okay." I made a sweeping gesture, as if to encompass all the years stretching ahead of him. "You know. In the broad scheme of things."

He offered me a wry smile. "I'm sorry I was an asshole."

"And I'm sorry I got you a bit part in a movie." I dropped him a wink and we laughed, standing to say our goodbyes.

"Best of luck to you, Maisie. I'll never forget what you've done for me. I hope you know that." Collin offered me his hand and then seemed to think better of the idea, pulling me in for a brief hug instead.

"You take care of yourself," I said, after he stepped back. "You're on a wild ride. Let it shock you each and every day. Promise me you'll stay flabbergasted."

He nodded, shoving his hands into his back pockets. "Each and every day." He gave a decisive nod then walked out of my office, pausing in the doorway to flash me a smile that somehow made me feel like he was going to be all right.

THIRTY-FOUR

Caleb

LIVING WITH MAISIE WAS EASY. She slid into my life like she had always been there, bringing the light right back with her. The water sparkled again. The volume was turned back up. Anything and everything was better with her around.

She hadn't found a job that called to her yet, but it turned out between her savings and mine—plus the considerable amount of stock she owned in Shift— there wasn't a whole lot of pressure on her to settle on something that wasn't a good fit. She spent a couple weeks running tours with me and was a wonderful asset, her vibrant personality playing nicely off my low key style. But Maisie needed something of her own. I knew that much.

One bright July day, Wyatt and Lucas asked me to come to The Hut for a meeting. When Maisie and I arrived, Cat and Kara swooped Maisie off—one of them leaning in to ask, "Are you really friends with Collin West?" I watched them disappear around the corner in a cloud of celebrity-fueled fandom, then headed to the office, where my brothers waited for me. Lucas managed to look commanding from his place behind the desk and Wyatt stood behind him, his back to me as he stared out the window.

"I thought I was coming in to talk with my brothers." I pulled out a chair and took a seat across from Luc. "Somehow this seems more serious than that." The atmosphere almost reminded me of being called in to talk with Dad, and I didn't like that. Not one bit.

Both my brothers bobbed their heads, and their solemn moods set off a little blast of nerves in my stomach. "We need to talk to you about something," Lucas said as Wyatt pulled up a chair to sit beside me.

"It's kind of a delicate matter," he added.

I sat up a little straighter, running through every possible delicate matter I could think of, and came up with exactly nothing. "Okay..."

"Do you remember when you were in here a

couple months ago and we told you the hotel was doing better than we could have hoped?"

I nodded and Lucas took over where Wyatt left off.

"Well, that's even more true now than it was then." A broad grin broke across his face, one that echoed my own. It felt good, knowing the family business was doing well. "And I'm sure you remember how much The Hut was involved with charities and stuff when Dad was around."

Dad's philanthropy was the one decent thing he did, though I still swore Mom had a lot more to do with it than she let on.

"Well, now that we have a handle on how to run things around here, we'd like to continue that Hutton tradition." Wyatt leaned forward, his gaze on mine. "And maybe even expand on it a little."

"That sounds wonderful." Happiness lightened the stress in my stomach. I missed knowing our success meant other people had a better chance, too. "But I'm still not seeing how any of this is a delicate matter."

"Prepare yourself." Wyatt sat back in his chair, visibly readying himself to drop a bomb. "The person who keeps coming to mind to run with that project is Maisie. She has the energy. And the drive."

I straightened enthusiastically. The idea couldn't have been more perfect. "She's always wanted to devote herself to helping people."

"Exactly." Lucas sat back, crossing his ankle over his knee.

My brothers' solemn moods still didn't compute. They were going to offer the woman I loved her dream job, and somehow they weren't comfortable with things? "I really don't see what's delicate about any of this. Maisie will be thrilled."

Lucas cleared his throat and rubbed a hand across his mouth. "Well, you see...if she took the job, she'd be tied to our family in a pretty permanent way."

And still. I wasn't seeing the problem. Because of me, Maisie had always been tied to our family. If recent events hadn't made that clear, I wasn't sure what would. "Yeah? So?"

My brothers exchanged an exasperated look. "Are you really going to make us spell this out?" Wyatt asked.

"Apparently I am. I can't come up with one good reason why Maisie isn't already tied to our family in a *pretty permanent way*." I lowered my voice, widening my eyes and waving my hands as I mimicked their word choice.

Wyatt eyed me like I might be stupid. "What if you guys don't work out, Moose? What if this burns hot and fast and she's out of your life just as quickly as she fell into it?"

I laughed, finally understanding my brothers' trepidation. "That's funny. I didn't even think about her leaving because...well...it's just not gonna happen. I figured you two, of all of us, would understand that, after how you met your wives. When it's real, you know."

"That's true." Lucas nodded his agreement with my statement. "But how could we know what you know, considering you haven't said anything? We'd be fools to presume."

"Presume away." I shifted a little to reach into one of the pockets on my cargo shorts and pulled out a black velvet box, which I opened to reveal the diamond solitaire nestled inside. I set it on the table. "I've had this for the last week. I just keep waiting for the right time and nothing seems appropriate yet."

A small gasp sounded in the doorway and I whirled to find Maisie standing there, with Kara, Cat, Harlow, and Mom behind her. All five women had their hands to their hearts or their mouths and one of my brothers let out a low groan while the other murmured, "Shit, Moose. Sorry about that."

Maisie stepped into the room. "What did you just say?" Joy twinkled in her eyes and she had never looked so beautiful. Not once in all the years I had known her.

I let out a long sigh and swiped the box off the desk. "Well, I guess the right time has just made itself known, hasn't it?" I crossed the room, my focus on this woman who had meant the world to me for as long as I could remember. "Or maybe every time was the right time, because ever since you bounced into my life with pigtails, freckles, and the brightest smile I ever saw, I belonged to you. My love for you goes beyond these last few months, beyond *now*. It extends through my life, touching everything I ever said and did, and everything I ever will say and ever will do. I'm going to marry you, Maisie Brown." I licked my lips as I repeated the promise I'd first made to her when I was six years old. "If you'll have me."

Without breaking eye contact, I plucked the ring from the box, ignoring the excited gasps and squeals coming from the doorway, and held it out to the woman I always knew would be my wife.

Maisie beamed and her eyes glistened as she nodded her assent. "It's about time you made good on that one." She stepped close and held out her hand while I slipped her ring in place. "Making a girl wait so long is kind of ridiculous, don't you think?"

I cupped her face between my hands and stared into her radiant blue eyes. "You know what they say about good things."

Maisie swallowed around a throat thick with emotion. "Totally worth the wait."

THIRTY-FIVE

Maisie

I NEVER THOUGHT I'd feel excited to see the house I grew up in. Of course, it wasn't going to be a house much longer—if it ever really counted as one in the first place.

Caleb pulled me close as a bulldozer trundled down the driveway. "You doing okay?" he asked. "It's not too late to back out. You have, maybe, thirty more seconds to change your mind before things go too far."

"I'm beyond okay." The bulldozer jerked to a stop in front of the rickety steps, the ones I could still hear creaking under my weight. "I always said that place needed to be wiped off the face of the earth. It feels damn good to be the one making the call to do it."

Caleb nodded, his eyes locked on the construction crew. "I'm surprised your parents didn't want to be here."

"They're not the ones with the ghosts that need exorcised." I jerked my chin toward my childhood home and the future site of The Reversal of Fortune Foundation—a non-profit organization geared toward helping under privileged children not just survive, but thrive.

My new passion project.

Not only was it everything I ever wanted, but as the CEO—a title that was a little grandiose, considering how small things were at this point—I would have the ability to ensure it stayed everything I ever wanted.

Caleb remained at my side as the little house was demolished. Maybe he thought I would fall apart a little, as this chapter of my past finally came to a close, and for that, I loved him all the more. We had grown up with him protecting me from things that hurt me, and while I was strong enough to stand on my own now, the two of us together made for an unstoppable force.

WORD about the foundation traveled fast, thanks to a little nudge from Collin West and a tweet from a budding starlet who exploded onto the scene shortly after I left Los Angeles. Instead of the quiet little inauguration ceremony we intended when we first came up with the idea, we were now having a full-on banquet, hosted by The Hut, with a star-studded guest list, and none other than Collin West himself playing in a very intimate setting. Needless to say, tickets were in demand and the price continued to climb.

Much to the family's amazement, Collin opted to stay at The Hut. Caleb and I were in the office with his brothers, working through a few last-minute details when Collin walked through the front door with his guitar slung across his back—a full hour early. He paused as one of Harlow's melodies filtered in from the kitchen, tilting his head so as to angle his ear toward the sound.

I bounded out of my seat. "Collin!" I cried as I made my way to him.

He waved a hand at me, closing his eyes and deepening the angle of his head. "What is that?" he asked, just as the melody stopped. "Damn it, Brown. You scared it away."

He glanced up as Harlow emerged from the back, guitar in hand, shock spreading across her features. "That was you?" he asked, pointing her way, oblivious to the rest of the family standing awkwardly behind him, gaping at the man who was fast becoming a legend.

Harlow nodded, looking almost apologetic. "Yeah, that was me. I'm sorry. I didn't think you were coming for another hour or I wouldn't have been playing when you got here." Mortification spread across her face as she realized that *the* Collin West had just heard her playing his favorite instrument.

"No." Collin shook his head and took a step toward her. "No way. Don't ever apologize for that." He turned to me. "Does she sing? Come on, Brown. You gotta tell me she sings."

"I'll let you find that out for yourself." I wrapped him in a hug. "How you doing?" I asked. "Still flab-bergasted?"

His eyes jerked immediately back to Harlow. "So fucking flabbergasted."

THAT NIGHT, the grounds of The Hut crawled with people dressed in tuxedos and cocktail dresses. Candles lined the walkways and strings of lights swirled down palm trees. The sunset gifted us with a glorious display and Collin sang like the angel Harlow thought he was. Caleb and I danced, swaying in time to the music, hidden amongst a cluster of couples. I pressed my cheek to his chest as little rockets of joy went off in my heart.

"Can you believe this is our life?" I asked. "It's perfect."

Caleb pulled away to look me in the eyes. "It's *almost* perfect," he corrected. "There are still a few items on my list that need checked off, thank you very much."

I beamed up at the man I had loved for my entire life. "Like what?"

"You still have the wrong last name, for one. And for two, we have a family that needs starting."

"A family..." His words hit a spot in my heart I didn't know existed. "I think I like the sound of that."

"I thought maybe we could start trying tonight." Caleb held me close. "And the next night. And the next. And the next night after that..."

I laughed as he paused, then surprised me by stepping out of my arms.

"There you are!" he exclaimed, his attention on someone behind me. I turned to find a dark-haired man, tuxedoed, smiling, and headed right for us. "Where have you been?" Caleb continued, holding out his hands and shaking his head. "You've missed just about everything. Literally everything."

The man ducked his head and brushed off the statement with a light shrug. "Like I said, I've been busy, Moose."

"Well damn it, Eli. How busy can you be?" Caleb wrapped his brother in a bear hug, thumping him on the back. "I swear, I was starting to think you were mad at me."

"Not mad. Just..."

"Busy. Yeah. You said that." Caleb took my hand and drew me into the conversation. "You remember Maisie, don't you? I figured, you know, since you're my brother and she's about to be my wife, it was damn near time you two finally met."

Eli's warm brown eyes lit up when they settled on mine. "Look at you! Little Maisie Brown, all grown up and hanging out with superstars. Sounds like life has been really good for you."

"Oh, believe me. It has." I shot him a look. "Which you'd know if you'd been around. Like at all."

His eyes went wide before he broke into laughter as I gave him my best smile. "You're fun. She's fun, isn't she?" He turned to Caleb. "We're gonna like having her around."

"We sure are." Caleb nodded, then put a hand on Eli's shoulder and leaned in close. "But again, I feel it's important to point out that the optimal word is *around.*

As in, if you pull another disappearing act, you'll never know how fun she is."

AS THE EVENING drew to a close, the Hutton family gravitated together, dropping into seats around one of the many tables and swapping stories of the evening. Everyone congratulated me on the roaring success on the inauguration of the foundation.

"Never, in my wildest dreams, did I think it would start off with such a bang." I stared in shock at the people surrounding me—the people who would soon be my family. "Thank you all for celebrating it with me."

Conversation moved on. Lucas picked on Eli for his disappearing act. Eli looked shocked to find out his mother had a boyfriend. Mrs. Hutton explained that she hadn't introduced said boyfriend tonight because she wanted to do it quietly, when just the family was around. Wyatt made a couple puns that had the table groaning and Caleb sat quietly, holding my hand and running his thumb across my knuckle.

"Since we're all here," Lucas began, then cleared his throat, "and it isn't exactly clear when that'll happen again." He gave a pointed look to Eli, who threw up his hands and made an exasperated noise.

"Wow, guys. I got it, okay? Having a life is forbidden in this family." He rolled his eyes and gave Harlow a strange smile that only I caught, as everyone else was giving their attention back to Lucas.

"Well," he began, beaming at Cat. "Family is exactly what I want to talk about. Because ours is expanding."

Cat nodded, placing a hand on her belly. "We just got the news, and I hate to take away from your day..." She glanced at me. "But...I'm pregnant."

Excited chatter filled the silence and Wyatt dropped a heavy hand on the table. "You're kidding, right?"

Lucas frowned. "Not exactly something we would joke about..."

But Wyatt was out of his chair, pulling Lucas into a tight embrace, thumping him on the back, then turning his attention to Kara, who looked just as dumbfounded as he did. "Because we just got the same news. Yesterday."

As the family digested the information, and Cat and Kara started trading specifics, Caleb squeezed my hand. "See," he whispered, "we're gonna have to get to work if we want to compete."

Mrs. Hutton sat back in her chair. "Two babies *and* a wedding? You boys are keeping me busy in the best possible way." She wiped at the corner of her eye and turned to Eli, who snorted and said, "Don't get your hopes up." and then Harlow, who blushed and looked away.

EPILOGUE

Maisie

"YOU GUYS really don't have to do this, you know." I looked at my two, just-starting-to-look-pregnant, almost-sisters-in-law.

"What are you talking about?" Cat asked. "Every bride-to-be deserves a bachelorette party."

"Right." Kara nodded her agreement. "And I didn't get one, so you have to let us take you out so I can live vicariously through you."

I turned to Harlow, who shrugged. "They have some kind of surprise in mind, that apparently only pregnant women are allowed in on. And even though I'm on the outside of this little circle"—she gestured at the two Mrs. Huttons—"I am in full agreement. Caleb finally proving he was serious about marrying you deserves some serious celebrating."

Following Cat and Kara's very specific demands, we had gone all out on clothes, hair, and makeup and as we piled into Cat's jeep, I had to admit we looked pretty amazing. The roof and doors were on this evening, to avoid ruining all our hard work. Cat's red hair flowed freely, while Kara's dark locks were piled into a messy up-do. Harlow had her white-blonde hair hanging in messy waves and had added a sultry shadow that made her blue eyes pop. I chose to wear Caleb's favorite dress, promising him before I left that when I got home that night, it would be right where it belonged—on our bedroom floor.

The music was on and the energy in the Jeep was high when we pulled into a parking spot in front of an unassuming building. Scrawled across the front was the word "Eggplant." Carloads of women poured into the lot, all of them dressed to kill and looking almost giddy.

"Eggplant?" I peered toward the door. "Where are we?"

Harlow gasped and repeated the name in horror while Cat and Kara unbuckled their seatbelts and turned to give me devilish looks. "It's a male strip club!" shrieked Cat, looking so over-the-top proud of herself.

Kara grinned. "It's like a who's who of romance book heroes. There are Vikings and Scots and business men and abs and skin...and they dance...*and* there's audience participation..."

"Guys..." Harlow sounded absolutely appalled. "We can't go in there."

Cat rolled her eyes. "Of course we can. The husbands and husband-to-be all know and gave their blessing on the occasion. We're not doing anything wrong...we're just...enjoying."

Kara bit her bottom lip. "And Maisie will enjoy things a little more than the rest of us because we signed her up for a chair dance with their lead dancer." Mischief did a saucy little tango across her face. "It's supposed to be incredibly erotic."

The two in the front seat squealed, then started climbing out of the Jeep while I tried to process where we were and what we were actually doing. "I hope you're kidding about that chair dance," I said as I swung my legs out of the vehicle.

"You'll thank us later." Kara grinned.

"And so will Caleb," Cat whispered.

Harlow still hadn't budged. "Guys...we really, *really* can't go in there." She shook her head, looking downright frantic. "I can't believe this is actually happening. Please get back in the car. We can go anywhere else."

"I'm actually surprised." Cat shifted her weight into her hip and frowned up at Harlow. "You're the last person I expected to get weird about a little male skin." She smiled to herself and waggled her head. "Okay, a lot. There will be a lot of male skin." A giggle devoured the end of her sentence

Harlow continued protesting even as Kara swung open her door for her and began assisting her exit from the vehicle. "Kara, stop. I'm serious. We just can't do this!"

Kara sat back on her heel and popped a hand on her hip. "Give me one good reason why we can't. This is the twenty-first century. We're allowed to express our sexuality now, you know."

"This has nothing to do with sexuality." Harlow let out a long sigh. "We can't go in there because Eli works here. *He's* the lead dancer."

Shocked silence settled on the group as we stared at Harlow with our jaws dropped.

"Eli works at Eggplant?" Cat turned toward the entrance as if somehow seeing the building would help it all make more sense.

"And he's the lead dancer?" Kara started giggling, her eyes on me as she realized just how surprising my chair dance would be—for everyone involved.

"I promised him I wouldn't tell, and so, you know, it would be really great if we could all just get back in the Jeep and find somewhere else to go." Harlow looked almost relieved as she finished talking.

"Oh, no." Cat shook her head. "There is no way we're *not* going in. He goes radio silent on us for months, hiding something like this"—she pointed at the purple neon eggplant on the door—"and you expect us to walk away?" She could barely finish the sentence because she was laughing so hard.

"She's right, you know." Kara managed through her giggles. "We can't pass up an opportunity like this. We just can't." She turned to me for support. "They don't do full nudity," she added, as if that made things all better.

"You know the guy better than I do, but if we go in there, I will *not* be the recipient of the chair dance. I just won't." It would have been bad enough if I wasn't connected to the dancer, but knowing he was my fiancé's younger brother...? There was just too much wrong with that thought to finish it.

And so, to Harlow's dismay, the four of us found our way into Eggplant, the den of decadent man-flesh, stopping on the way to make sure I wouldn't be the one heading onstage tonight.

We were, however, seated right down in front, where we had a clear view of the dancers—and the dancers had a clear view to us. As women all around us hooted and hollered, beautiful man after beautiful man made his way onto the stage.

Just as Kara promised, there were Vikings and Scots, men in fedoras, men in camo and dress blues, and there, right in front, wearing a kilt and so much body oil every single muscle flexed and twitched under the hot lights, was Eli.

Cat and Kara let out twin gasps of shocked appreciation, then lost themselves to a fit of giggles, while Harlow dropped her head into her hands.

Eli was good at what he did. Very, very good.

There was no denying the moment he recognized the four of us, tittering away in the front row. His eyes landed on mine, then bounced from Cat to Kara to Harlow, who mouthed an apology and held out her hands in an I-tried-everything-to-get-them-to-leave-and-I'm-so-sorry gesture.

With a crooked grin, and a twist of his head, he ripped off his kilt just as the bass dropped. While the four of us stared in shock, the crowd of women around us lost their collective minds.

———————————

THE GIRLS and I swore to Eli that we wouldn't spill the beans on his secret life on the stipulation that he would spill them all by himself. Soon. None of us were interested in keeping secrets from our husbands. Harlow apologized profusely to her brother who laughed it off, with a charming smile and shrug of his shoulders.

"It was gonna come out anyway. And I swear, seeing the look on your faces was probably the best possible way it could have happened." He laughed and that was that. Family crisis averted—at least until he told his brothers.

A few weeks later, Caleb and I were married in a beautiful ceremony. What we didn't have in peacocks, we made up for with love. He stared at me like I was an angel as I made my way down the aisle toward him. When I arrived, he leaned in to whisper, "I'm gonna marry you, Maisie Brown." And the words I'd heard so many times in my childhood brought tears of happiness to my eyes.

Shortly after that, surrounded by family and friends, he made good on his promise.

Mom and Dad were there, looking better than they had in a long time. Dad swore he hadn't touched a drink in the last six months and never would again. It was the same tune he'd sung for me countless times, but something about this felt different. For the first time in a long time, I had hope for them. It was, after all, a day for making good on lifelong promises.

I used to think that reversals of fortune were the

best kind of stories, but staring into my husband's eyes as he slipped his ring onto my finger, I changed my mind.

The best kind of stories were the ones like ours.

THANK YOU FOR READING CALEB & Maisie's story! I fell in love with their sweet, genuine love for each other. I hope you did, too.

Are you ready to fall in love with the sexy-strutting, Eggplant-working Eli Hutton? Click here!

READY FOR MORE RIGHT NOW? Turn the page for a quick peek at the pact Eli Hutton's signed with his roommate, Hope Maxwell.

PART ONE

BEYOND US SNEAK PEEK

THE PACT

This agreement is made by and among the roommates named herein who have signed a lease for a shared dwelling unit that makes the roommates jointly liable for all terms of the contract.

The amount of alcohol imbibed while drawing up this contract does not make it any less binding—even though neither party is a lawyer and cannot state this fact with any degree of accuracy.

I, Hope Maxwell, do hereby solemnly swear that by entering into this roommate agreement with Eli Hutton, absolutely no hanky-panky of any kind will exist between us, because there will never be an *us*. While we live together, all feelings of attraction will be expressly ignored, and our friendship will remain strictly platonic. In the case of accidental nudity, any desire that arises will also be ignored. (Which will be easy because I'm sure no desire will arise at all as I am swearing off men for the rest of my life. As handsome as Eli is, as glorious as he's sure to be sans clothing, he's like a brother to me. I'd rather claw my eyes out than see him naked.)

I, Eli Hutton, do hereby solemnly swear that by entering into this roommate agreement with Hope Maxwell, absolutely zero physical shenanigans will happen between us. I further agree that anyone who becomes part of an *us* is a fool because relationships devour souls. For the duration of our cohabitation, I will not look at Hope as anything but one of the guys and in the case of accidental nudity, ~~she will consider herself very lucky~~ I will politely cover my goods and never speak of the incident. (And we all know she'd love to see me naked. No clawing of eyes would happen. I promise.)

Neither "She Who Will Not Be Named" nor "He Who Can Burn In Hell" will be discussed, as those ~~mistakes years of torture~~ *relationships* are over and both Hope and Eli are better off without them. Speaking either of those names may summon them back from the pits of hell and no one wants to be responsible for what happens after that.

If Eli considers entering into another relationship— whether with "She Who Will Not Be Named" or otherwise—Hope promises to hit him upside the head with a frying pan, stop baking delicious treats, and remind him what happens when he invites jealous, gold-digging, nagging women into his life. (Except for Hope of course. Hope is an angel and is welcome to stay as long as she likes.)

If Hope considers entering into another relationship—whether with "He Who Can Burn In Hell" or otherwise—Eli promises to sit her down with a carton of ice cream, walk her through what happens when she allows men to put their needs above hers, and remind her to do her homework, as college is no longer on the backburner now that "He Who Can Burn In Hell" is gone.

No jokes will be made at Eli's expense regarding his place of employment and the fact that half his family still doesn't know he dances mostly naked for crowds of women. He will tell them on his own time, when he feels it's appropriate, and will not tolerate anyone sticking their nose into this business. (I'm serious, Hope!) (Gosh, Eli! I get it. It's totally up to you to decide when to tell your brothers.)

No jokes will be made at Hope's expense regarding the fact that she attends college online because she didn't want to take classes with a bunch of eighteen-year-olds who might call her old.

All rent will be paid on time by both parties. Utilities split equally. Living spaces must be kept neat, blah, blah, blah and yada, yada, yada.

Any deviation from this agreement will signify the end of this friendship. The guilty party will relinquish any claim on the apartment and quietly remove him/herself from the premises.

Signed, toasted, and agreed upon by two questionably tipsy new roommates.

Hope Maxwell

Eli Hutton

———

Ready for more? Click here!

ACKNOWLEDGMENTS

So many people come together to bring my books into the world.

Thank you to my husband, for *Top Gun* quotes and belly-bursting laughter. Thank you for deciphering my poor tongue-tied words when I try to communicate. (Why can't I just write everything??) Thank you for showing me what true love feels like. For so many missed connections that led to perfect timing. You are proof that magic exists and I love you more with each passing day.

Thank you to my children. You guys give me purpose. Watching you grow from teeny little erratic people into bigger, less erratic people has been a joy. All joking aside, I respect the people you're becoming and even though you will never read this note, because you will never read this book, because I'm your mom and that might be a little weird, I need you to know the following:

I love you.

I'm proud of you.

I thank God for bringing you into my life.

Your names are written in gold across my heart.

Thank you to Joyce, Linda, Jackie, and Nickiann. Your support over the years has been FABULOUS. Go team Brooks!

And finally, thank you to Fleur, Vanessa, Katherine, Kieran, Nicole, Zuleyka, Stormi, Cynthia, Vickie, Darlene, Stephanie, Kris, Elaine, Maria, Cali, Ashely, Jennifer, Amanda, Jennie, AnneMarie, & Joanna.

LOVE YOU ALL.

Books by

ABBY BROOKS

STANDALONES

It's Definitely Not You

The Hutton Family

Beyond Words

Beyond Love

Beyond Now

Beyond Us

Beyond Dreams

Brookside Romance

Wounded

Inevitably You

This Is Why

Along Comes Trouble

Come Home To Me

A Brookside Romance - the Complete Series

Wilde Boys Series with Will Wright

Taking What Is Mine

Claiming What Is Mine

Protecting What Is Mine

Defending What Is Mine

The Moore Family Series

Finding Bliss

Faking Bliss

Instant Bliss

Enemies-to-Bliss

The London Sisters Series

Love Is Crazy (Dakota & Dominic)

Love Is Beautiful (Chelsea & Max)

Love Is Everything (Maya & Hudson)

The London Sisters - the Complete Series

Immortal Memories

Immortal Memories Part 1

Immortal Memories Part 2

As Wren Williams

Bad, Bad Prince

Woodsman

Connect with
ABBY BROOKS

WEBSITE:
www.abbybrooksfiction.com

FACEBOOK:
http://www.facebook.com/abbybrooksauthor

FACEBOOK FAN GROUP:
https://www.facebook.com/
groups/AbbyBrooksBooks/

TWITTER:
http://www.twitter.com/xo_abbybrooks

INSTAGRAM:
http://www.instagram.com/xo_abbybrooks

BOOK+MAIN BITES:
https://bookandmainbites.com/abbybrooks

Want to be one of the first to know about new releases, get exclusive content, and exciting giveaways? Sign up for my newsletter on my website:

www.abbybrooksfiction.com

And, as always, feel free to send me an email at: abby@abbybrooksfiction.com

Made in the USA
Monee, IL
06 February 2021